WALT DISNEY

THE JUNGLE BOOK

THE STORY OF WALT DISNEY'S
MOTION PICTURE

THE
JUNGLE
BOOK

AUTHORIZED EDITION

RETOLD BY MARY CAREY

Adapted from the Mowgli Stories
by Rudyard Kipling

WHITMAN PUBLISHING COMPANY • RACINE, WIS.

CONTENTS

About This Book

Long, long ago, Rudyard Kipling wrote some marvelous tales about a little boy named Mowgli, who was raised in the Indian jungle by a pair of wolves. Mowgli, who was called "man-cub" by his animal friends, was very happy in the jungle with his wolf parents and his wolf brothers. For Mowgli liked to believe that he was a wolf.

This is a new story about Mowgli, and a different one from the tales by Kipling. It is based on the Walt Disney animated film *The Jungle Book,* and it tells of Mowgli's adventures with Bagheera, the stuffy panther; Baloo, a very swinging bear; and Shere Khan, the tiger who hated man.

The story for the motion picture is by Larry Clemmons and Ralph Wright. Terry Gilkyson and Richard M. and Robert B. Sherman wrote the songs. The film was directed by Woolie Reitherman, and the designs for the characters are by Ken Anderson.

1.
Bagheera the Panther

BAGHEERA, the black panther, could hear the young wolves when he was still some distance away.

"They're playing again!" Bagheera said to himself. He found the thought most disturbing. Play was all very well for tiny cubs, little balls of fur with eyes hardly opened to the world. But Mother and Father Wolf's family were no longer little balls of fur. They were half-grown young wolves. They should be learning to run with the pack. They should be learning to hunt, to keep downwind of their prey. Yet there they were in the clearing near their den, yipping and scuffling like mere puppies, running to and fro and making such a din that the birds flew up from the trees shrieking in protest.

"Most improper!" was Bagheera's comment. "All Mowgli's fault!" And, having put the blame exactly where it belonged, the panther continued on toward the wolves' den.

As he went, his nose told him that a deer had just passed this way. The information did not interest Bagheera. He had fed well the night before, and now he was moved only by curiosity. He wanted to see what the young wolves were doing.

It was nearly sunset when Bagheera reached the clearing near the den. Mother Wolf and Father Wolf were there, resting under a great tree at the edge of the jungle and watching their young. They acknowledged Bagheera's arrival with a glance. The panther settled himself near them, curled his tail around his body cat fashion, and watched, too.

There was a game going on, no doubt about that. It was a noisy, running, sliding, tumbling, dodging game. The object, as nearly as Bagheera could make out, was to nip an opponent in the leg, then run away without being nipped in return. Four young wolves raced this way and that, their pink tongues lolling out and their white teeth snapping. They chased each other furiously, always attacking from the front. A fifth player went about the game a little differently. When an opponent rushed at him, he would leap over the other's back, then spin about, nip quickly at a hind leg, and dance off. The fifth player was Mowgli, the man-cub, and he nipped not with his teeth but with his fingers.

"They're frightfully noisy," said Bagheera after he had watched the play for some minutes.

"It's a game Mowgli thought of," said Mother Wolf proudly.

"I guessed as much," said Bagheera. Always it was Mowgli thinking of new things, as if a man-cub—or a wolf—couldn't get into enough trouble just going about his business in the usual fashion.

"Mowgli is cleverer than the others, I think," said Father Wolf fondly.

"Perhaps that's because Mowgli is a man-cub and not a wolf," Bagheera reminded them thoughtfully. "He is different."

The remark should hardly have been necessary.

11

Certainly Mother Wolf and Father Wolf knew this as well as anyone.

"He is my cub," said Mother Wolf. "I carried him home from the man-village myself."

Bagheera had heard the story a hundred times. Now he had a sinking feeling that he was about to hear it for the hundred and first time. He was right.

"It was when Shere Khan hunted here," said Mother Wolf dreamily. "The people in the man-village had shut themselves up inside their walls for fear of Shere Khan. They had left my little Mowgli alone in a field, forgotten, and even though he was screaming, no one came out to get him. They were afraid!"

Bagheera made a sympathetic noise in his throat. Leaving a tiny man-cub alone in a field was hardly the thing to do. Still, he could understand the fear of the villagers. Bagheera was a mighty hunter, but even he stepped aside when his path crossed that of Shere Khan, the tiger.

"No one went to the man-cub but me," continued Mother Wolf. "When he saw me, he wasn't a bit frightened. He stopped screaming and put his little hands up to my face."

"And so nothing would do but you had to pick him

up and carry him home with you," finished Bagheera dryly.

Mother Wolf's eyes flashed and the fur on her neck rose. Bagheera remembered suddenly that in her youth she had been called Raksha, which means "The Demon."

"What else could I do?" she demanded. "Could I leave him to be eaten by Shere Khan?"

"Oh, no!" said Bagheera hastily. "Of course not. You did the only right thing!"

But in his heart Bagheera did not believe this. Just what the proper course of action was when one found a man-cub abandoned in a field, he did not know, but it seemed to him that adopting the little creature was a rather extreme way to remedy the situation.

And where would it end? Perhaps one day Mowgli might run with the wolf pack, but he would never *be* a wolf. The game in the clearing was proof of that. It was Mowgli, the man-cub, who had coaxed his wolf brothers to play. It was Mowgli who had made them forget the watchfulness that should be their nature. Why, they had not even noticed Bagheera!

"Mowgli should go back to his own people," Bagheera thought. But he was careful not to say this aloud.

He did not want to offend Mother Wolf a second time.

"See how quick Mowgli is," said Father Wolf.

"He is quick," Bagheera admitted. There was not a mark on the man-cub's skinny legs. Not once had he been caught by one of his brothers. He was laughing, pushing his black hair out of his eyes, watching his chances, then darting in to pinch and dart away again. Bagheera felt a reluctant pang of admiration. Then he reminded himself that to be quick might not be enough in the jungle. Ten times the rains had come and gone since Mother Wolf had carried Mowgli to her den, and still he was but half-grown. It would be many seasons more before the man-cub was truly a man. Would Mother Wolf and Father Wolf live to see this? If not, who would protect Mowgli? What would become of him?

"He should go back to his own people," thought Bagheera again.

At that, Mowgli, running from one of his brothers, caught his foot in a vine and tumbled head over heels toward Bagheera, tossing dust and dried leaves into the panther's face.

"Bagheera!" Mowgli saw the panther looming over

him and scrambled to his feet. "I'm sorry, Bagheera," he said. "I didn't see you."

Bagheera shook his head and sneezed the dust from his nostrils. "I know, I know," he said. "You should be more careful, man-cub. Suppose Shere Khan, the tiger, had been sitting here watching you?"

Mowgli's chin went up defiantly. "Shere Khan hunts in the north," he declared. "Besides, my father and mother would never let Shere Khan come so near. And . . . and I am not afraid of Shere Khan!"

"That's because you're a foolish man-cub," said Bagheera. "And it is indeed fortunate for you that Shere Khan does hunt in the north, for he would—"

But Father Wolf interrupted. "Listen!" he said.

From beyond the trees came the cry of Akela, the leader of the wolf pack. He was calling his followers to him!

2.
Council Rock

AKELA SAT in the moonlight at the very top of Council Rock and watched his pack assemble. First to answer his call were the elders. As was their right, they grouped themselves in a half-circle behind Akela. Then they waited. They were the old wolves, patient and wily, cunning hunters who held the memories of many a chase through the jungle night. Like Akela, they were the guardians of the law of the pack. Many, like Akela, had muzzles touched with the frost of years. Like Akela, they were strong and wise. But none were as strong and as wise—or as old—as Akela.

After the elders came the hunters, male and female. They were younger, these runners with the wind, and were longer of breath, perhaps, than the elders. But they still had to learn the lessons that only time can teach. They took their places facing Akela, looked up to him, and were still.

Behind the hunters came the mothers with their cubs. Among these were Mowgli and his brothers, quiet for once while at the side of Mother Wolf.

Last to come was Bagheera. For many seasons the black panther had joined in the councils of the wolf pack. But Bagheera remembered always that he was a guest. Stepping delicately, careful not to disturb any of the wolves, he circled the mothers and their young, passed the hunters, and took his accustomed place almost hidden in the shadows behind the elders. There he crouched, motionless.

When all were ready, Akela spoke.

"Shere Khan is returning."

Akela said it simply and quietly—as simply and quietly as it could be said—but a ripple of uneasiness swept through the pack. Behind Akela, even the elders stirred and shifted. Bagheera, of course, did not deign to move even a whisker, but he looked to the place where Mowgli sat close to Mother Wolf and he felt a coldness gather about his heart.

"Shere Khan is returning," repeated Akela. "The ravens have seen him journeying from the north, and they flew to us to tell of it. And this morning Akil overheard the bandar-log in the trees chattering of a bullock killed near a pond not two days from here."

"Should we worry about the monkeys' chatter?" said one wolf, one of the hunters. "Their heads are empty."

"Their heads are full enough today," replied the wolf named Akil. "They can talk of nothing but how mighty Shere Khan is. They watched him pull down the bullock and kill it with one blow. Then he fed."

"He will travel slowly then," said another wolf.

"But he *will* travel," Akela pointed out. "He is coming."

On the fringes of the pack, the mother wolves looked nervously at their cubs.

"But why should we care?" said one wolf, whose name was Nadan. He was a young hunter who had not yet taken a mate. "Hasn't Shere Khan hunted among us before? Bagheera hunts among us, and he sits with our councils. There's enough game for all of us."

One of the elders got up and came forward to stand beside Akela. "Nadan, do you remember Shere Khan?" he asked the young wolf.

"No," admitted Nadan. "But I've heard my mother speak of—"

"You've heard your mother speak of the days when the tiger hunted as we do," interrupted the elder. "But have you heard how Shere Khan broke the first law of the jungle?"

The young wolf had not.

"Your education has indeed been neglected," said the elder severely. "Shere Khan hunted man. What's more, he hunted in the fields on the very edge of the man-village. It was a foolish thing to do. Naturally the men came out with their guns. They carried their red flower blooming on the ends of long sticks. One of the men threw a stick, all burning with the red flower, and it struck Shere Khan in the face. I did not see it, but the monkeys shrieked of it for days afterward. They said the tiger screamed. Then the men pointed their guns and there was a great noise, and Shere Khan screamed again and ran away, and his blood dripped on the ground as he went. Ever since then, Shere Khan has hated man and man's guns and man's fire!"

"But what is that to us?" said young Nadan. "We are not men."

The old wolf looked beyond Nadan and beyond the other hunters. He looked at Mowgli, huddled close to Mother Wolf. Then all the wolves turned to follow the old one's gaze.

Mother Wolf, finding every eye upon her and her man-cub, came bristling to her feet. "Shere Khan will not harm Mowgli," she vowed. "He is my cub!"

"He is a man-cub," said Akela.

"He is mine," declared Mother Wolf.

"That may well be," Akela said, "but he is a man— or he will be someday. Shere Khan will seek him out. You know this is true. The tiger has tried it before."

Mother Wolf held her tongue, remembering how Shere Khan had come to her when first she carried Mowgli from the man-village. He had demanded the man-cub, and when she had refused, he had tried to push his way into her lair. Fortunately, the way had been too narrow for the tiger, and Raksha had flown at him, her teeth flashing. In the end, Shere Khan had gone away. But, Raksha recalled, he had gone growling threats at every step.

Mother Wolf felt Mowgli next to her. He was trembling ever so slightly. Still, he stood strong and straight.

"I will keep him safe," Mother Wolf promised. "He can stay inside the den. Shere Khan cannot get in there."

Behind Akela, Bagheera smiled in the darkness. How like Mother Wolf. She would keep the man-cub with her, even if it meant hiding him in a hole in a rock for the rest of his life.

"Mowgli is no longer a tiny cub, unable to crawl," Akela reminded Mother Wolf. "He cannot spend his life in a den like some kind of grub who hides from the sun. There is only one thing to do."

The wolves waited.

"Mowgli must go back to the man-village," said Akela.

"Ah, yes," said Bagheera to himself. "Yes, of course. That's how it goes. Leave it to Akela."

But Mother Wolf cried, "No!"

And Mowgli, next to her, cried out, "No! No, I won't go!"

Akela looked sternly at the man-cub. "You are only

a cub," he told Mowgli. "You may not speak at the council."

"But I am a wolf!" cried Mowgli.

"Be quiet!" said Akela.

"Mowgli, be still," his mother said gently. Then she turned to Akela as Father Wolf came to stand with her. "If Shere Khan tries to take Mowgli," she declared, "he will have us to deal with."

"And you will die," Akela said simply.

It was true. Mother Wolf knew it, and she was silent.

Bhera, a young wolf, then spoke up. He was a big, broad-chested hunter, braver than he was cunning, perhaps, but very strong. He had never failed in the hunt since he began to run with the pack. "Mowgli is one of us," he pointed out. "Long ago he was taken into the pack. How can we send him back to the man-village? We must keep him with us, and we must protect him from Shere Khan."

Akela shook his head. "Would you stand against Shere Khan?" he asked the young one.

"Why . . . why, yes, of course," said he.

"Then you would die, too," Akela said. "None of us is a match for Shere Khan. We are strong, but he is stronger. We are quick, but he is quicker. There is no other way. I say that Mowgli must go back to his own people. He will be safe there. If he stays here, even if Raksha can hide him from Shere Khan, the tiger will get his revenge. There are other cubs in the pack besides Mowgli. They are the ones who will pay if Shere Khan becomes angry."

At this there was a murmur among the mothers. Several of the males left the hunters and came to their mates and their cubs. Raksha, the fierce one who could face Akela without flinching, the one who could drive Shere Khan away from her den, wilted as the others gazed at her.

"We have a day's time before Shere Khan comes," said Akela. "Perhaps, with great good fortune, we have two. No more than that, and that is little enough. If the man-cub leaves immediately, he will be safe in the man-village before Shere Khan can learn of it."

"No!" shouted Mowgli again. "Not the man-village! I won't go!"

"Hush, Mowgli!" cautioned Mother Wolf.

"What does the pack say?" cried Akela.

No one answered for a moment. Then one of the elders, the one who had told of Shere Khan's hunting and his encounter with man's red fire, stepped to the top of Council Rock. "He must go!" declared the old wolf.

Below him, the other wolves took up the cry. "He must go! He must go! Back to the man-village!"

Mowgli trembled and buried his face in his mother's fur so that none could see the tears in his eyes. Bagheera, still silent behind the elders, felt a pang of pity. The wolves were casting the man-cub out. It was the only sensible thing to do, of course, but what a shame that there was not an easier way.

At last the wolves were quiet, and Akela sealed the verdict with the words, "It is decided then, little one. You will go, and our thoughts will go with you. May you find happiness among your own people."

"But . . . but *you* are my people," sobbed Mowgli.

"Not anymore," said Akela sadly, and he turned as if to leave the council.

"Wait!" cried Mother Wolf. "We have not finished."

"Oh?" Akela returned to his place. "The pack has decided," he told her. "Mowgli must go to the man-village. What more can be said?"

"But how?" demanded Mother Wolf.

"How?" echoed Akela.

"How?" murmured the elders behind him.

"Why, he must walk, of course," said Akela reasonably. "How else? It is not so far. He can make the journey easily in two days if he goes quickly."

"Alone?" demanded Raksha. "He is still a cub. As you say, he is too young to speak at the council. He is also too young to travel for two days alone in the jungle."

Having delivered this statement, Raksha sat down beside Mowgli. There was a trace of a smile at the corners of her mouth, but she was careful to keep her head down so that Akela would not see it. "There is more than one way to catch a rabbit," Mother Wolf told herself.

"I had thought . . ." said Akela, hesitating a little, "I had thought that *you* would. . . ."

"I cannot go," said Raksha firmly. "There are my other cubs—Mowgli's brothers. Who would look after them if I went off to the man-village?"

Father Wolf stepped forward, about to say that he would guard Mowgli on the journey. But his mate caught his eye and her glare reminded him that he, too, was a responsible creature who could not leave

27

his family to traipse off to the man-village. "I would be happy to go with Mowgli," he said weakly, "but my young will go hungry unless I hunt for them."

Akela looked then to the hunters. His eye fell upon Bhera, the brave young one. Bhera had boasted that he would defy Shere Khan. Let *him* take the man-cub.

But no. Bhera would never do. Anyone foolish enough to speak that way of the tiger would be far too foolish to guide the man-cub to the village. He would doubtless be shot before he got within miles of the place. Besides, judging from the set of Mowgli's chin and the way the man-cub clenched his fists, getting him to the village would be a task for the wisest among them.

"Perhaps," said a soft voice behind Akela, "perhaps I may be of help." And Bagheera, the panther, stalked forward.

Akela was surprised. Seldom did Bagheera speak up at the council, and when he did say anything it was usually because he had been asked a question. The courtesy of the panther was flawless. He never interfered in the affairs of the wolves.

"I go where I wish," said Bagheera, "and unless I wish it, no one sees me."

"We know that," Akela agreed.

"I have been to the man-village many times," Bagheera told the wolves. "Not once have the men come rushing out with their guns and their red flower, for the very simple reason that they did not know I was there. I cannot take the man-cub into the village; none of us can do that. But if you will permit it, I can take him to the place where the river runs down through a field and the jungle ends. From there the man-cub can see the wall man has built around his village, and he can go on safely alone."

Akela felt a surge of relief. Raksha had asked a difficult question for very obvious reasons. Now, for some quite obscure reason of his own, wily old Bagheera was answering it.

"We will permit it," said the wolf gratefully. "And we thank you, Bagheera. But why?"

"Why am I doing it?" asked Bagheera. "Because it must be done, that's why. The man-cub belongs with his own."

But Bagheera looked at Raksha. The she-wolf was standing with her head lowered. In her eyes was a look that Bagheera had never seen before. It was not anger. It was something far, far beyond anger. Bagheera

29

turned away from her and addressed the others.

"I will come here to get the man-cub," said Bagheera. "I will come in the morning."

And he went swiftly away from Council Rock.

3.
Kaa the Python

THE NEXT day, Bagheera was quite disinclined to present himself to Mowgli's family. The journey to the man-village would be long, he knew, and a good start in the freshness of the early morning was certainly indicated. Besides, the longer he delayed, the greater was the chance that they might meet Shere Khan upon the way. Still, he did not want to face Mother Wolf. Not quite yet. "Wait a bit," he told himself. "When Raksha has had time to consider the matter, she'll see that we are doing the best thing. The only safe place for the man-cub is back with his own people."

So Bagheera sent word by Lak, the raven, that he would come for Mowgli after the heat of the day had passed. Then the panther settled himself in the lower branches of a tree and slept uneasily while the sun journeyed across the sky. When at last the shadows on the jungle floor were long and cool, Bagheera made his way to Council Rock. The start of the journey could be delayed no longer.

But Bagheera had not reckoned on the wolves—or on Mowgli. The man-cub could not leave without embracing each of his wolf brothers in turn. And once he had done this, he went back and did it all over again, as if to be sure it was done properly. Then, of course, Mowgli had to take his leave of each member of the pack, and even old Akela had come to bid him farewell. This took a remarkable amount of time, and even when it was over, Mowgli was not ready. He had to say good-bye to Father Wolf, who was so overcome with grief that he was quite speechless, and to Mother Wolf, who had just remembered numbers of pieces of good advice which she had to give to her man-cub before he left her. He must remember to examine his feet carefully every day, she told him, to make sure he had not picked up a thorn which might fester. He must hold his head high when he went into the man-village, so that they would know that Raksha's cub was among them.

Bagheera growled deep in his throat to remind everyone that the sun was getting very low. At this, Mowgli clasped his mother around the neck and buried his face in her fur.

"I don't want to go!" he wailed.

"You must go, Mowgli," said Mother Wolf. "The pack has decided. It's the only way."

Bagheera sighed with relief. He was pleased to hear that Mother Wolf recognized this. That was good.

But still Mowgli clung to her, and still she spoke to him, very softly, like a mother comforting a tiny cub.

It was Akela who settled the matter at last. He came to stand next to Mother Wolf and the man-cub. He said nothing, but she met his gaze and gently put Mowgli away from her.

It was over, and Mowgli knew it. He turned to join Bagheera, and together the panther and the boy went down the hill toward the edge of the forest. Once

Mowgli looked back. The wolves were motionless on Council Rock—all except his mother. She had followed a little way, but when she saw Mowgli watching she stopped and sat down.

"Come along, man-cub," chided Bagheera. "Don't lag behind. It will be dark soon."

Then the jungle closed around them. Council Rock and the pack werę gone.

For a time Bagheera and Mowgli traveled in silence, Mowgli going as slowly as he possibly could, stopping to kick at leaves and twigs on the path. Several times Bagheera had to sit down and wait for the boy to catch up with him.

"Good heavens!" he said. "At this rate, we won't be at the man-village before the next rains!"

Mowgli did not answer, and he walked no faster.

"Come, come, man-cub!" said Bagheera. "You'll like it there in the man-village, once you get used to it."

"I'm not going!" announced Mowgli.

"Of course you're going, man-cub," said the panther. He was determined not to lose his temper, and he resisted the temptation to cuff the boy around the ears. He stopped and looked about. The sun was gone now, and the floor of the jungle had become very dim.

"Getting dark," said Bagheera.

Mowgli said nothing.

"We'd better sleep in a tree tonight, eh, man-cub?" suggested Bagheera.

Still Mowgli said nothing, so Bagheera selected a fine tree with a huge, sturdy trunk. "Up you go!" he commanded.

"But I don't want to go back to the man-village!" Mowgli protested, as if the hated place were perched in the upper branches of the tree.

Bagheera ignored this remark, which really had nothing to do with where they would spend the night. "Now come on up this tree," he coaxed. "It'll be safer there."

Mowgli looked up. Thirty feet above him a great limb jutted out from the trunk. "Way up there?" the boy asked.

"That's right."

Mowgli had learned numbers of things from his wolf family, but climbing was not one of them. He could manage fairly well on a tree small enough so that he could get his arms around the bole, or one whose branches reached low to the ground, but one this size hardly seemed possible. Still, he did not want to admit to Bagheera that there was anything he could not do. He took a short run and jumped, clawing at the bark of the tree, digging in with his toes and knees, and removing quite a bit of skin from his shins.

"Ha!" snorted Bagheera. "Is that all the better you can climb?"

"It's too big around!" protested Mowgli. "Besides, I don't have any claws."

"And well do I know it," was Bagheera's dry comment. The big cat put one paw under Mowgli's rump and pushed, climbing easily as his claws took sure, quick hold of the bark. "Up you go!" said the panther, generously overlooking the fact that Mowgli seemed determined to kick at his ears. To himself Bagheera muttered, "Helpless man-cub!"

When they had reached the lofty branch, Bagheera watched Mowgli settle himself against the bole of the tree. "Now get some sleep," the panther told the boy. "We've got a long journey ahead of us tomorrow."

Bagheera stepped delicately past Mowgli, gave a prodigious yawn, stretched once or twice, kneading the branch with his claws just to keep in trim, then put his head down on his forepaws and closed his eyes.

Mowgli watched Bagheera for a few moments. To all appearances the panther had dropped off to sleep instantly and completely.

"I want to stay in the jungle," said Mowgli.

Bagheera's whiskers twitched, but he didn't bother to open an eye. "You wouldn't last one day," he mumbled.

"I'm not afraid," said Mowgli. "I . . . I can look out for myself!"

Bagheera didn't answer. Mowgli threw himself back against the tree, scowling, and suddenly found himself staring into a pair of eyes—strange, yellow, very cold eyes.

It was Kaa, the python, who had come silently, by what road only Kaa knew, and now was coiled around the tree limb just above Mowgli's head.

"S-S-S-Say now!" hissed Kaa. "What have we here?"

The snake's head came very close to Mowgli's face, and the flat, ugly nostrils seemed to be sniffing. The forked tongue darted in and out, tasting the air. "It's a man-cub!" chuckled Kaa. He was quite delighted. "A delicious man-cub!"

Mowgli did not like this at all. He had heard stories

about Kaa and about what befell those who were unfortunate or incautious enough to meet the snake and look into those cold yellow eyes. If Mother Wolf had been there, Mowgli would have run to her. But she was not there, and Mowgli had just declared that he could take care of himself.

"Go away!" said Mowgli. He put his hand against Kaa's nose and pushed—hard. "Go away and leave me alone!"

Bagheera, stretched out on the branch nearby, heard the words through a fog of sleep. "I should go away," he muttered wearily. "I should go and leave you. But I won't. Now please go to sleep, man-cub."

"Ah, yes-s-s!" hissed Kaa, ever so softly. "Man-cub, please go to s-s-sleep! Sleep, little man-cub, s-s-sleep!"

Mowgli looked again into the deadly eyes. He would tell Kaa again to go away. But he found that he could not. His own eyes opened wide, staring, fixed in the gaze of the snake. He felt that the tree was moving, up and down, up and down, like the water in the stream near Council Rock. He was moving, too—floating, swirling along with a current, sinking, and then coming to the surface again. And it was so easy! There was no need to swim. The water would carry him, hold him. He could go on forever in the stream, floating with Kaa!

Coils touched Mowgli's throat, then wrapped around his body. He did not notice. It was too pleasant in the stream, floating through the jungle. There was no man-village. There would never be a man-village.

Then Kaa tightened his grip, and Mowgli was drowning. His breath went out and the stream was gone, and there was the night and the darkness and Kaa. And beyond, on the branch, was the panther.

The python shifted, relaxed its grip on Mowgli for a moment—only a moment. It was long enough. Mowgli drew a single breath and cried out.

"Bagheera!"

"Confound the man-cub!" thought the panther. "Will he never let me get any rest?"

"Now, look," he said, not turning around, "there's no use arguing anymore. Now, no more talk until morning!"

Mowgli did not answer, but another voice did. "Ahhh!" came Kaa's evil whisper. "But he won't be here in the morning."

Instantly Bagheera was up and wide-awake. He saw Kaa. And he saw the man-cub, whom he had sworn to protect, helpless in the python's coils.

"Kaa!" roared Bagheera. A huge black paw lashed out, smashing the python's head against a branch.

"Ahhh!" groaned Kaa. The snake forgot completely about Mowgli. He shook his head to clear it of mists, relaxed the coils which held the man-cub, and turned a glare of pure hatred upon Bagheera.

"Ahh, Bagheera! You have just made a very serious mistake!" warned Kaa.

"Now, now, Kaa!" said Bagheera in what was meant to be a friendly tone. Like most jungle creatures, Bagheera would go miles out of his way to avoid meeting Kaa.

"A very s-s-stupid mistake!" hissed Kaa.

Bagheera felt an explanation might help. "Now," he began, "I was just—"

"Look me in the eye when I'm speaking to you," commanded Kaa.

That was exactly what Bagheera was trying to avoid. "Now, just a minute, Kaa," he protested, trying to shrink away from the snake.

"In both eyes," insisted Kaa. "If you please."

Bagheera did not please, but he found that he could not help himself.

"You have just sealed your doom!" Kaa told him in a horrid whisper.

Unable to speak or move, Bagheera could only stare, entranced.

"Your doom!" repeated Kaa.

Bagheera watched Kaa's great head come closer . . . closer . . . until the yellow eyes filled the whole world.

Then, quite suddenly, Kaa was gone! There was a crashing from below, a moaning, and Mowgli was slapping Bagheera on the jaws, begging the panther to wake up.

"Eh?" Bagheera came to himself, shuddering violently from head to tail. "What? What?" he demanded. "What happened?"

"Kaa was all curled up on the branch," Mowgli explained brightly. "I shoved his body off while he was looking at you, and his head went after the rest of him. Look down there, Bagheera!"

Bagheera looked down. Pythons are almost indestructible, but Kaa was much the worse for wear. Even he had to feel some effects after dropping from a thirty-foot branch. He was hissing and moaning, struggling to straighten out his coils and regain some of his icy dignity.

41

"Look, Bagheera," laughed Mowgli. "He's got a knot in his tail."

It was true. The python glared up at them. "Just you wait!" he threatened.

Mowgli laughed again, but Bagheera warned him sharply to be still. The two watched as the snake crawled painfully away, groaning and threatening.

"He won't be back tonight, at any rate," said Bagheera, much relieved.

"Not with a knot in his tail," giggled Mowgli. Then the boy saw Bagheera's stern face and his laugh trailed away.

"So you can look out for yourself in the jungle, can you?" demanded Bagheera.

"I pushed Kaa off the branch, didn't I?" said Mowgli. He had really expected praise for the deed, not a tiresome harangue about his helplessness.

"Would you have had a chance to do that if you'd been alone?" asked Bagheera.

Mowgli was silent.

"You still want to stay in the jungle, do you?"

"Y-Yes," said Mowgli. "I want to stay in the jungle."

"Ha!" snorted Bagheera. And, "Huh!"

The panther turned away from Mowgli and stretched out once more, settling to sleep. He gave one last "Huh!" before he said softly, pleadingly, "Now *do* go to sleep, please, man-cub!"

4.
Colonel Hathi's Troops

BAGHEERA wakened with the confused impression that the world was falling to pieces around him. Or, if not falling to pieces, it was certainly shaking a great deal. Or, if not the world, at least the tree in which Bagheera and Mowgli were sheltered was not behaving as one had a right to expect.

Bagheera opened his golden-green eyes and looked around him. On every side leaves were dancing in time to a steady crashing, tramping sound that came from the jungle floor. Not only the leaves were dancing, but the branches and even the huge bole of the tree vibrated to the regular count of "Hup . . . two . . . three . . . four!"

"Oh, no!" groaned Bagheera. "It's the dawn patrol!"

The panther twitched in annoyance. Mowgli, who had been comfortably curled up with his head on Bagheera's hindquarters, roused himself and sat up to rub the sleep from his eyes.

"Keep it up!" came the command from below. "That's it! In step now! Hup . . . two . . . three . . . four!"

"Bagheera, what's that?" asked Mowgli.

"Hathi," said Bagheera shortly.

"Hathi?" Mowgli leaned out and looked down through the foliage. On the ground below he could see a gigantic old bull elephant marching along, stamping mightily at every step. Behind the big bull a herd marched in single file, each one stamping in perfect rhythm with the old bull and with each other. Last in the line was a very young elephant calf. The thunder of the big ones shook the forest and made Mowgli bounce on his tree limb, but this little one was no earth-shaker. He tried to keep in step, but every few moments he had to break into a half-run or be left behind the others.

Mowgli pointed to the old bull. "Is that Hathi?" he asked.

"Colonel Hathi," said Bagheera, "and don't you forget it!"

"He has two names?" Mowgli had never heard of such a thing before.

"Hathi is his name," said Bagheera. "Colonel isn't really a name. It's a man-word, and it means 'leader.'"

Mowgli was satisfied for the moment, and Bagheera began to ready himself for the day, licking his paws and rubbing them down over his face and up behind his ears. Bagheera was not much interested in Hathi and his herd. He only regretted the thoughtlessness that had permitted him to choose a tree above the elephants' parade ground for his resting place. Soon, he comforted himself, the elephants would march off and he and Mowgli could go on with their journey.

"Why does Hathi use a man-word with his name?" asked Mowgli.

"He says that they made him Colonel Hathi in the army," Bagheera answered.

"The army? What's an army?"

"It's something you'll learn about someday," said Bagheera, "when you're in the man-village."

Mowgli was confused. If he had to learn about the army in the man-village, it must be a man-thing. Then what had an elephant bull to do with it?

"Did they make him Colonel Hathi a long time ago?" asked Mowgli.

"A very long time," said Bagheera, and he added, "if they ever did." But he said this very quietly, for Mowgli was just a cub, and it is not always wise for cubs to know too much about their elders.

Bagheera knew Hathi's story. It had been whispered to him by his father, who had gotten it from *his* father, who had it from *his* father, who had learned it from a rather garrulous and dim-witted old cow elephant. Hathi had never really been in the man-thing called an army. He called himself "Colonel" and he put on great airs, but everything that he knew about the army he had learned from an old bull who had, indeed, been a cavalry elephant in Her Majesty's service—until he had run off to the jungle to spend his last years regaling whoever would listen with tales of battles and marches, parade grounds and drills and inspections. Hathi had listened and remembered, and, because an elephant's life is long and he was the oldest of his herd, everyone believed Hathi now. Sometimes he even believed himself.

Below Mowgli and Bagheera, the elephants did a lumbering about-face at Hathi's command. The little calf skipped nimbly out of the way and marched along beside them as Hathi shouted, "Sound off!"

Ten trunks were raised in the air and ten elephants trumpeted loudly.

"Very good," said Hathi. "All together now!"

> "Oh, the aim of our patrol
> Is a question very droll,
> For to march and drill
> Over field and hill
> Is a military goal!"

sang the elephants.

"Pick it up!" shouted Hathi. "Pick up the speed. Hup . . . two . . . three!"

"What are they doing that for?" asked Mowgli.

"I suppose," said Bagheera, "that they're doing it because Hathi thinks it's a good idea."

"I bet I can do it," was Mowgli's reply.

Bagheera started to tell Mowgli that he had neither

the nose nor the bulk to join an elephant herd, but he didn't have time. He had scarcely gotten a word out when Mowgli grasped a vine and swung down toward Colonel Hathi's herd.

"Mowgli!" cried Bagheera. "Come back here!"

Mowgli paid no attention. He hit the ground running, and he didn't stop until he had skidded into hiding behind a huge fern. From this shelter he watched the troop march by. They were all perfectly immense, and it was obvious even to Mowgli that none would be at all inclined to stop and welcome him to the group. But there was the calf, skipping behind the others. Mowgli waited until the little one came abreast of him. Then he slipped out and joined the march. "What are you doing?" he asked.

"Shhh!" said the baby elephant. "We're drilling."

"Can I drill, too?" asked Mowgli.

"Sure. Do what I do. But don't talk in ranks," warned the youngster. "It's against regulations."

Mowgli accepted the reproof and fell into line behind the elephant calf. He bent until his hands touched the ground, and, as he went along, he swung to and fro as the others were doing. If he could not stay in the jungle as a wolf, thought Mowgli, why not join Colonel Hathi's herd and stay as an elephant?

"To the rear, march!" shouted Hathi.

The obedient elephants swung about.

"The other way!" whispered Mowgli's little friend. "The other way! Turn around! Quick!"

Mowgli reversed direction in time to keep himself from being trampled, and for a few marvelous moments he strutted at the head of the line of elephants. But then, "Hup . . . two . . . three . . . four . . . to the rear!" roared Hathi.

Again the elephant troop turned about. Mowgli continued straight on alone for a few steps before he realized his mistake, spun, and ran back to join the herd.

"Companeeey—halt!" barked Colonel Hathi.

Everyone but Mowgli stood still as a statue. Mowgli bumped into the baby elephant.

"Halt means stop," said the little one, not unkindly.

"Companeeey—left face!" ordered the colonel.

The elephants swung about and stood in a straight line facing the colonel, who began to pace up and down, swinging a twig back and forth in his trunk.

"March, march, march!" Mowgli heard someone mutter. It was the fourth elephant down the line—

a matronly creature with perhaps a bit more spread in the middle than is necessary even for an elephant. "My feet are killing me," she complained.

The young bull standing next to her blew softly through his trunk. "I'm sick of it," he told her. "I'm putting in for a transfer to another herd."

"Silence in the ranks!" cried Colonel Hathi. He glared at the two grumblers, and they snapped to rigid attention.

"Dress up that line!" commanded Hathi.

Ten pairs of eyes shifted to left and to right as the line was dressed up. The baby elephant lined his trunk up with the treelike leg of the elephant next to him. Mowgli, not having a trunk to line up, hastily abandoned his elephant stoop and stood upright next to his young friend.

"Inspection!" announced Colonel Hathi. "Present arms!"

Ten elephants extended ten trunks stiffly in front of them. "Stick out your nose!" the baby elephant whispered.

Mowgli tried, squaring his shoulders and shoving his face forward. "Like this?" he asked.

The little elephant didn't think it was much of a

nose, but he was too polite to say so. "That's right," he encouraged Mowgli.

There was no time to say more, for Colonel Hathi was coming down the line, pausing here and there to tell one elephant to straighten up and warn another not to get vines tangled in his tusks. *"Esprit de corps,"* Hathi lectured his troop. "That's the important thing. That's the way I earned my commission in the Maharaja's Fifth Pachyderm Brigade."

Mowgli was aware that the stout elephant fourth down in line seemed to sigh slightly.

"Back in 'eighty-eight, it was ," Hathi went on. "Ah . . . or was it?"

"Here it comes," whispered the stout one. "The Victoria Cross bit again!"

"It was then I received the Victoria Cross," blustered Hathi, "for bravery above and beyond the call of duty!"

There was an almost imperceptible sagging of the line of elephants, and of this the colonel was magnificently unaware. "Those were the days!" he said. "Discipline—discipline was the thing!" He paused to clear his throat. "Build character and all that sort of thing, what?" He paused, reminiscing.

No one answered, and the old bull suddenly pulled himself up short and came back to the present. "Ha!" he snorted. "Yes . . . ah . . . where was I? Oh, yes. Inspection."

Down the line he came again, glaring in a military fashion at one after another of his troop, and at last reaching the baby elephant.

"Let's keep those heels together, shall we, Son?" he cautioned gently.

The baby shifted his weight and obligingly planted one front foot almost on top of the other. "Okay, Pop, sir," he said happily.

Hathi's eye fell upon Mowgli. "Well," he trumpeted, "and what have we here?"

Mowgli pressed his heels as tightly together as two heels could be, pushed his shoulders back still more stiffly, and raised his nose still higher into the air.

"Eh?" said Colonel Hathi. "I say! What's this? A man-cub?"

Mowgli had been hoping against hope that Hathi would think he was an elephant—a very small elephant with a very short trunk. It was instantly clear that Hathi thought no such thing, for the big bull snatched Mowgli up, lifting him in his trunk until the boy could look squarely into Hathi's little eyes. Mowgli did not like what he saw in those eyes.

"This is treason!" shouted Hathi. "Sabotage! I'll have no man-cub in my jungle." And he emphasized the point by slamming Mowgli to the ground so violently that the boy's ankles seemed about to come up through his shoulder blades.

It took Mowgli a moment to get his breath, but once he had it he turned lustily to the attack. "This is not your jungle!" he shouted at Hathi.

"Silence!" bellowed Hathi. He was very angry. His first instinct was to crush the impudent man-cub with one blow of his trunk. Fortunately for Mowgli, Hathi remembered in time that he was supposed to be Colonel Hathi, late of the Maharaja's Fifth Pachyderm Brigade. "You are under military arrest," he said coldly.

Mowgli didn't have the faintest idea what this meant. Neither did Bagheera, who had watched the whole affair from the tree. But Bagheera knew the time had come for him to take a hand. "Just a minute, Hathi!" he cried.

Like a black streak, Bagheera was down out of the tree and racing toward the outraged elephant. "Hold it, Hathi. I can explain," he began.

"*Colonel* Hathi, if you please!" said the old bull.

"Yes, yes, of course! Colonel Hathi." Bagheera bowed his head to acknowledge his breach of manners. "The man-cub is with me," he explained. "I'm taking him to the man-village."

Hathi looked from Bagheera to Mowgli, then back to Bagheera. "Will he *stay* in the man-village?" he wanted to know.

"Why, of course . . ." Bagheera began.

"But I'm not going!" Mowgli interrupted. "I'm not—"

A cuff from Bagheera shut off Mowgli's protest. "You have the word of Bagheera," the panther assured the elephant.

That was good enough for Hathi. "Very well," he told Bagheera. He swung his great bulk around and lumbered off, muttering into his trunk about young whippersnappers. "Let's get on with it!" he shouted to his troops. "Right face! Forward march!"

The elephants faced right and marched off—all except the baby, who had something to say to Mowgli, something special enough to make him momentarily deaf to his father's military commands.

"I'm sorry," the little one told Mowgli.

"That's . . . that's all right," Mowgli answered. "I guess I really wouldn't make much of an elephant."

"Your nose *is* awfully short," the baby agreed. "I don't suppose it will grow much?"

"I don't suppose so," said Mowgli.

"Too bad," said the youngster. "Mine will. And when I grow up I'm going to be—"

Mowgli was never to learn what the baby would be when he grew up, for the stout lady elephant fourth in line among Colonel Hathi's troops discovered at just that moment that the herd was short by one very young calf. She called the matter to the colonel's attention in no uncertain terms, and Hathi took prompt action.

"To the rear, march!" he thundered.

Having given what he considered was the correct order, Hathi momentarily abandoned his role as army colonel and became a father. He sped past his marching troops, scooped his son up in his trunk, and began a monumental lecture. "If I've told you once, I've told you a thousand times . . ." he scolded.

"Pop, look out!" cried the little one.

The marching elephants, accustomed to following orders, marched on. "Pop!" shouted the baby. "Say halt! Say halt!"

It was too late. The marchers tramped down upon their colonel. Bagheera scarcely had time to snatch Mowgli out of the way before Colonel Hathi went down, his son still held in his trunk. Then the elephant who had collided with the colonel was trying to struggle out from beneath the elephant who had marched behind him, and the third elephant in line found himself pushed by the fourth, and in seconds the entire herd was down in a shrilling, trumpeting tangle of legs and trunks and tusks.

Mowgli laughed.

"It's not funny!" snapped Bagheera. The panther might not believe all of Hathi's tales of grandeur in the Maharaja's Fifth Pachyderm Brigade, or of courage beyond the call of duty, but he had a profound respect for Hathi nevertheless. The old bull might never have been in the man-thing called an army, but he had held leadership of his herd for longer than Bagheera could remember, and it was sheer insanity to insult him.

"Man-cub," said Bagheera in his chilliest tone, "what you have done this morning is to show once again that the jungle is no place for you. You've been extremely rude to Hathi. Remember, he could step on you with no more trouble than it would take to . . . to step on that beetle over there. Now, come along. Let's get away from here before something else happens."

Mowgli looked around and saw that Colonel Hathi was struggling to his feet. The man-cub had no real desire to look again into Hathi's tiny, white-fringed eyes, and he gladly followed as Bagheera sped away.

The panther and the man-cub ran, Bagheera covering the ground in long strides and Mowgli loping behind, using the easy half-run he had learned from his wolf brothers. When the sounds of the elephants had faded behind them, Mowgli felt it might be safe to ask a question. "Bagheera," he cried, "where are we going now?"

They had reached the edge of a small stream. Bagheera answered without even looking around. "You are going to the man-village," he declared. "Right now!"

A tree had fallen across the stream, bridging it. Bagheera leaped onto the tree trunk and crossed the water without breaking his stride. Mowgli stopped suddenly and backed away from the tree. "I'm not going!"

"Yes," said Bagheera. "You are!"

"I'm not!"

Bagheera turned about and started back across the

log. "You are going if I have to drag you every step of the way," he told Mowgli.

But if Bagheera was determined, so was Mowgli. The boy wrapped his arms around a slender sapling that grew beside the stream and announced, "I'm staying right here."

Bagheera wondered for the hundredth time what madness had made him volunteer to take the man-cub to the village. This sort of behavior was outrageous. Bagheera would not stand for it—not for a moment.

"You are coming with me!" he growled, his voice taking on an ugly edge.

"I'm not!"

"Let go of that tree!" Bagheera's teeth closed on the loincloth around Mowgli's waist. "Let go!" snarled the panther through clenched jaws. He braced with all four feet and tugged.

"I won't!" cried Mowgli. "I won't! You let go of me!"

Bagheera only tugged harder.

Still clinging to the tree, Mowgli doubled up, planted both feet firmly against Bagheera's muzzle, and pushed.

Bagheera felt cloth slipping between his teeth. He

felt, with shock, Mowgli's hard little heels digging into his jowls. There was a ripping, a scrabbling for a foot-hold on the muddy stream bank. Then the panther tumbled backward, clawing at the air. The stream closed over him and the current bumped him against stones before he could struggle to the surface, blow the water out of his nose, and blink it out of his eyes. He found a slippery footing on the stream bottom and glared at the bank, where Mowgli still clung to his tree.

"That does it!" roared Bagheera.

The panther padded out of the stream, trying to look as dignified as possible, while shaking the water from his pelt. "I've had it!" he gasped. He was so angry that he could scarcely breathe. "You want to be on your own?" he demanded. "Well, you've got your wish. From now on, you're on your own—alone!"

With that the panther leaped to the low-hanging limb of a big tree and disappeared into the jungle.

"Don't worry about me," said Mowgli. But there was no one to hear him. Bagheera was gone!

5.
Baloo the Bear

THOUGH Bagheera had walked on noiseless feet, his going seemed to leave the jungle terribly quiet. Mowgli noticed for the first time that there was no wind. The leaves had stopped whispering in the trees. Not a ripple disturbed the grasses on the forest floor. Except for a far-off splashing from the place where the stream tumbled down a tiny gorge, it was completely silent.

"I can take care of myself!" shouted Mowgli.

Not even an echo came back.

"I guess I showed him," said Mowgli, more softly

now. "I showed everyone!"

There was no one to argue this or to ask exactly what it was that Mowgli had showed Bagheera and everyone. Mowgli drooped. Defiance was useless when there was no one to defy.

The man-cub sighed, sat down with his back to a large boulder, and began to trace aimless circles on the ground with a bit of twig. He should, he knew, look about immediately for a den. A dry, sandy cave in a hillside—one with a narrow mouth to keep out unwelcome visitors—would be perfect. Yes, he must find such a den. Yet he felt strangely unwilling to move. The big stone at his back seemed comforting somehow. Nothing could come upon him from behind as long as he stayed here.

Above him, a bird suddenly shrieked and flew off. Mowgli started, dropping his twig.

Something was coming! Mowgli heard twigs snap and the sound of branches being brushed aside. Kaa! Was it Kaa, writhing through the underbrush, thirsty for his revenge on the man-cub? But no. Even with a knot in his tail, the giant python would go more quietly.

The noise came closer, and Mowgli thought of Shere

Khan. His mouth went dry. But Shere Khan's claws were sheathed in velvet. It could not be the tiger wallowing about in dry leaves like a water buffalo in a pond.

Then Mowgli heard the singing. The words made no sense to the man-cub, no sense at all, but the voice made Mowgli think of thousands of honeybees swarming about their combs.

"Doo-be, doo-be, doo-be, dee-doo!"

sang the unseen one, crashing nearer to Mowgli.

"Well, it's a doo-bah-dee-doo.
Yes, it's a doo-bah-dee-doo.
I mean a doo-bah-dee-doo!"

Mowgli couldn't decide whether to run or to stay where he was.

"Doo-bee-doo-bee, doo-bee, de-doo!"

continued the singer.

The branches near the stream heaved. It was too late to run. Whatever the creature was, it was there!

With a final "doo-bee-doo!" it burst into the open.

Mowgli's mouth fell open. It was a bear! It was a

stout, shaggy, baggy bear. As bears sometimes do, he was walking on his hind legs. Walking was perhaps not the right word. He was dancing, taking little jigging, skipping steps in time to his "doo-bee-doo's," swinging his very ample hindquarters, and switching his stub of a tail at every step.

His bright, black little eyes fell upon Mowgli, and the singing and dancing stopped together.

"Well, now," he rumbled, "what have we here?"

It was a friendly enough question, but Mowgli did not answer. Truth to tell, the man-cub was badly frightened, but he did not want to show it, so he stuck out his lower lip, pulled his eyebrows down in a fierce scowl, and tried to look much more ferocious than it is really possible for a rather skinny man-cub to look.

The bear refused to be discouraged. He simply set about answering his own question in his own way— with his nose. He put his huge head down next to Mowgli's small one and sniffed a mighty sniff.

"Hum?" he said. And, "Hey!" And, "What a funny little bit of. . . ."

Mowgli slapped at him. "Go away!" he cried.

The bear reared back. "Oh, boy!" he chuckled, not a bit angry. "I've seen everything in these woods." He put his head to one side and considered Mowgli cheerfully. "What a pretty thing this is!" he decided.

Mowgli stood up. "Leave me alone!"

"Well, now!" The bear tapped Mowgli on the shoulder. "That's pretty big talk, Little Britches."

Mowgli had been called a foolish man-cub often enough by Bagheera. He had had to put up with it. But "Little Britches" was too much. "I'm big enough!" he stormed, and he emphasized this by hammering the bear's rotund midsection with his fist.

"Ha-ha!" roared the bear. Then he sobered momentarily, shook his head, and remarked, "Pitiful! Kid, you need help!"

This took Mowgli by surprise. "I do?" he asked.

"You sure do," said the bear, "and old Baloo's going to teach you to fight like a bear."

"You are?"

The bear stepped back, assumed a fighting stance with his front paws held high, and began to dance again. But this time there was no song. "First comes the footwork," Baloo told Mowgli. "Keep moving! Come on, kid!"

Mowgli doubled his fists and raised his arms stiffly in front of him.

"Yeah, yeah!" applauded Baloo, leaping nimbly around. Mowgli aped him, dancing as he danced.

"All right, kid," pleaded Baloo. "Loosen up! Get real loose and then start to weave."

Baloo demonstrated and Mowgli weaved, skipping back and forth. Once he dodged in under Baloo's paws to land a punch on the bear and then slipped away. It was like a game, thought Mowgli. It was like the game he had played with his wolf brothers.

"That's it!" cried the bear. He stopped dancing and bent toward Mowgli. "Now give me a big bear growl," he commanded. "Scare me."

Mowgli screwed up his face, bared his teeth, and growled. It was the best the man-cub could do, but it was not much of a growl as growls went in Baloo's circle. It set the bear to laughing.

"No, no!" cried the bear. "Boy, I'm talking about a *growl!* Like a *bear!* A *big* bear!" Baloo's huge chest swelled. His arms flexed. His head went back and his mouth opened wide. And he growled a truly magnificent growl. He growled so mightily, in fact, that Bagheera, traveling through the trees far beyond the stream, heard him and froze in his tracks.

"Oh, good heavens!" thought the panther. "The

man-cub! He's in trouble!"

The frightful growling sounded again, as if to confirm Bagheera's fears.

"I shouldn't have left him alone!" the panther fretted. He turned and started back, racing through the trees. The growls continued, growing louder and more terrifying with every stride Bagheera took. "I'm too late!" thought the panther frantically. "What will Mother Wolf do when she finds out?"

More hideous growls rent the air.

"It's all my fault!" Bagheera told himself sternly.

The stream was just ahead, with its log bridge. Bagheera raced out onto a broad limb overhanging the water. He gathered his muscles for the leap that would carry him across the stream. His eyes flashed as he thought of what he would do to any creature who would dare to harm Raksha's cub. He would tear the enemy limb from limb. He would . . . he would. . . .

There was another bloodcurdling growl, and then a laugh. "Like that!" said Baloo. "A big one, right up from your toes!"

And Mowgli growled. It was not a very big one, but it did come right up from his toes. Baloo was generously inclined to give the man-cub credit for his good intentions. "Ha-ha!" he laughed. "Now you're getting it, kid!"

"Oh, no!" moaned poor Bagheera from his tree limb. "Baloo! Of all the creatures in this world, why did the man-cub have to meet that stupid, shiftless. . . ." Words failed Bagheera. With an exasperated sigh he settled down on the tree limb to see what Baloo and Mowgli were up to.

Having finished, for the time being, with the course in growling, Baloo returned to sparring, plain and fancy. "Weave about, now," he told the boy. "Loosen up! Light on your feet . . . that's it. Now look for an opening."

Mowgli looked and found one. He skipped in and punched.

"Now you're getting it!" chortled Baloo. "Ha-ha! Come on, that's it!"

Mowgli took another swing at Baloo. This time he missed.

"No, no!" laughed Baloo. "Not like that. Like this!" He tapped Mowgli lightly on the side of the head. To the bear it was just a love tap; Baloo felt that he had scarcely touched the man-cub. But Mowgli went spinning, stumbling, then falling against a log.

Bagheera cleared his throat. "Fine teacher you are, old ironclaws!" he said in his most cutting tone.

The irony was lost on Baloo, who looked up, gave the panther a friendly grin, and said, "Oh, thanks, Bagheera."

"Tell me," said Bagheera, "after you knock your pupil senseless, how do you expect him to remember the lesson?"

"Huh?" For the first time Baloo saw that Mowgli was indeed knocked senseless. "Well," said the bear, "I . . . I . . . well, I didn't mean to lay it on so hard."

Mowgli stirred, sat up, blinked, then struggled to his feet. "I'm not hurt," he insisted. He was staggering a bit. "I'm all right." Then, as if he was afraid that he wouldn't be believed, he declared, "I'm a lot tougher than some people think."

Baloo was greatly relieved. "You'd better believe it!" he said heartily. "You ready to go again?"

Mowgli nodded.

"Now I want you to keep circling, or I'm going to knock your roof in again," warned Baloo.

Mowgli began circling, fists up.

"Keep moving," instructed Baloo. "Watch for an opening."

Mowgli, his head clearing, watched and saw his chance. He darted forward and tapped Baloo on the nose.

"Oh!" cried Baloo. He had barely felt the blow, but he wanted to make Mowgli feel good. "Right on the button!" he applauded. Then he reeled, staggered, and fell.

Mowgli might be a novice at fighting with bears, but Baloo did not fool him for an instant. The man-cub knew the bear was playing. "Get up! Get up!" he shouted. He leaped onto Baloo's back, grabbed a handful of rough fur, and tugged.

"Ha-ha-hoo!" howled Baloo, going into a sudden spasm. "No! No! You're tickling!"

The bear rolled over and tried to bring his legs up under him to shake off the man-cub. Mowgli, delighted, refused to be shaken. He scratched at Baloo's shaggy sides, pulling the bear's loose pelt up and down over his ribs, while Baloo ho-hoed and ha-haed and howled and gurgled until he almost choked. "Now, we don't do that here in the jungle!" sputtered Baloo. "I can't stand . . . ha-ha-ha . . .no! Help! Help! Bagheera!"

"That's all the man-cub needs," sighed Bagheera.

"A little more confidence!"

"Give up, Baloo?" laughed Mowgli.

"I give up!" howled Baloo. "I give up! I tell you, I give up!"

Mowgli slid down off the bear, and Baloo sat up, trying to get his breath. "You . . . you know?" he gasped. "You know something?"

Mowgli shook his head.

"You're all right, kid," said Baloo warmly. "What do they call you?"

"They call him Mowgli," Bagheera put in before the man-cub could answer. This rough-and-tumble with Baloo had gone far enough, the panther decided. Too far, in fact. It never would have started if Bagheera hadn't lost his temper and left the man-cub alone. That wouldn't happen again. "He's going back to the man-village," announced Bagheera.

Baloo was shocked. "The man-village?"

Bagheera confirmed it. "Right now!" he said sternly.

"You've got to be kidding!" protested Baloo. "They'll ruin him. They'll make a man out of him."

Mowgli, who had wilted upon hearing Bagheera's words, brightened up immediately. "Oh, Baloo!" he cried. "I want to stay here with you!"

"Certainly you do!" agreed the bear.

"Oh?" said Bagheera. "And just how do you think he'll survive?" he asked Baloo.

Baloo plainly considered the question a gross insult. "What do you mean, how do you think he'll survive?" he growled. "He's with me, isn't he? And I'll teach him all I know."

"That shouldn't take long," snapped Bagheera.

It was intended as a withering comment, but Baloo didn't wither. Instead he turned his back on the panther and offered an enormous paw to Mowgli. The man-cub gladly took Baloo's paw in both of his hands. "Look, Little Britches," said Baloo, "it's like this. All you've got to do is look for the bare necessities."

"The bare necessities?" questioned Mowgli.

Baloo nodded wisely. Then, in his deep, rumbling voice, he began to sing:

"Look for the bare necessities,
   The simple bare necessities.
   Forget about your worries and your strife."

Baloo let go of Mowgli's hands long enough to dance in a little circle. Mowgli, delighted, followed suit.

"I mean the bare necessities
  Are Mother Nature's recipes
  That bring the bare necessities of life,"

sang Baloo. Then he demonstrated, picking up a coconut which had fallen near them. Deftly he cracked it, using his head instead of a stone. Then he gulped down the meat and sang:

"Wherever I wander,
  Wherever I roam,
  I couldn't be fonder
  Of my big home!
  The bees are buzzing in the tree
  To make some honey just for me.
  When you look under the rocks and plants
  And take a glance at the fancy ants,
  Then maybe try a few. . . ."

Baloo lifted a stone so that Mowgli could see the ants scurrying about underneath.

"You eat ants?" said the man-cub in wonder.

"You'd better believe it!" declared Baloo. He scooped up a generous clawful of the insects and popped them into his mouth. Mowgli, ready to try anything, managed to capture a single ant, but before he could get it to his mouth it had run up his arm and down his back and escaped. Baloo's methods of getting his bare necessities worked well for Baloo, thought Mowgli, but they didn't seem to do *him* a bit of good.

"The bare necessities of life will come to you," Baloo told him.

"But when?" asked Mowgli.

"They'll come to you," insisted Baloo. He took hold of the stem of a banana tree and bent the tree toward Mowgli. The man-cub suddenly found himself staring into a huge bunch of bananas. "Thanks, Baloo!" he said, picking one.

But when Baloo released the tree, the bananas snapped free. Mowgli was deluged with fruit!

"They'll come to you," repeated Baloo. Again he began to sing:

> "Look for the bare necessities,
>   The simple bare necessities.
>   Forget about your worries and your strife.
>   I mean the bare necessities.
>   That's why a bear can rest at ease,
>   With just the bare necessities of life."

Baloo danced up to a prickly pear bush and coolly removed three pears, unbothered by the bristling thorns which armored the bush. "Now, when you do this," he told Mowgli, "you've got to take care. Don't pick a prickly pear with your paw. Use your claw." As Mowgli watched, Baloo showed how it was done, using his long claws to avoid the prickles. Mowgli didn't attempt it. Unlike the bear, he had no claws.

"But," said Baloo, "you don't need to use claws when you pick the big papaws." He delivered a mighty thump to the bole of a papaw tree, and the fruit tumbled down into Mowgli's outstretched hands. "Have I given you a clue?" asked the bear.

"Golly," exclaimed Mowgli. "Thanks, Baloo."

"Oh, of all the silly nonsense!" growled Bagheera, who was still brooding in his tree.

"Aw, come on, Baggy," pleaded Baloo, "get with the beat." And the bear yanked at the panther's tail with such gusto that Bagheera almost fell out of his tree.

"The bare necessities of life will come to you!" sang Baloo.

"They'll come to you!" piped Mowgli.

"They'll come to you!" echoed Baloo.

Bagheera kept his frosty silence, so Baloo decided to ignore him. "Hey, Mowgli, how about scratching my old left shoulder for me, huh?" he said.

He crouched down so that Mowgli could reach his shoulder. The boy, only too happy to oblige, clambered up on his back and began to scratch vigorously.

"Now just a hair lower," said Baloo. "There! Right there! That's it! Ah!"

Mowgli went on scratching.

"Ah, beautiful!" rumbled Baloo. "Great, just great! This is living!"

But Baloo still wasn't satisfied. Not completely. "Kid, you've started something," he told Mowgli. "We've got to get to a tree. This calls for some *big* scratching!"

He waddled away from Mowgli, backed up to a rough-barked forest giant, and rubbed first his shoulder blades and then his hindquarters on the tree, groaning and muttering with pleasure.

"Ahhh!" he sighed. "Right on it! Yeah! That's delicious!"

Mowgli giggled. "You're lots of fun, Baloo!"

"Oh-hoo!" woofed the bear, too preoccupied with having a good scratch to give the compliment his full attention. And "Uh! Huh! Hah!" went the bear, rubbing his neck against the tree trunk. "Ooooh! Yeah!"

Mowgli was fascinated. He had seen wolves scratch, but never like this. Baloo made it seem a game, or perhaps more than a game. To Baloo, scratching was obviously one of the major pleasures of life. Mowgli tried it, rubbing his back on a small tree with comparatively smooth bark. It did feel rather good.

Now Baloo, limp with enjoyment, sagged away from his tree and let himself slide lazily down the stream bank and into the water. "Just try to relax," rumbled the happy bear. "Yeah, cool it!" He floated on his back, drifting slowly toward the middle of the stream.

Mowgli was not about to lose sight of his wonderful new friend. He skidded down the muddy bank and plopped into the water.

"That's it!" encouraged Baloo. He scooped the man-cub out of the river and set him high and dry atop his big shaggy chest. "Fall apart in my backyard," invited Baloo.

Mowgli accepted the invitation, stretching his full length on Baloo and staring down into the bear's face. A bee buzzed by, intent on some errand of its own.

"Let me tell you something, Little Britches," said Baloo. "Don't act like that bee acts, 'cause if you do, you're working too hard."

Bagheera, ignored and completely forgotten, muttered, "Lazy, shiftless, good-for-nothing bear!"

"And don't spend your time looking around for something you want that can't be found," continued the bear, who was now floating downstream with the current. "You'll find out you can live without it, and you'll go along without thinking about it."

"I give up!" groaned Bagheera. "I just hope the man-cub's luck holds out."

The panther stayed where he was, brooding on the injustice of it all. Throughout the journey he had acted only for the man-cub's good. No one could deny that. And what thanks did he get? None! None at all! At the first opportunity Mowgli was going off with that ne'er-do-well Baloo. And what could come of that? Baloo would spoil the man-cub even more badly than Raksha had. And if danger threatened, the empty-headed old bear would probably be off robbing a hive somewhere, and a fat lot of good he would be to Mowgli.

"I can't help it," said Bagheera sadly. "I tried. And

that's all anyone can ask for."

Mowgli's high, thin laugh sounded as he and Baloo drifted out of sight around the bend of the stream. "Baloo, I like being a bear!" cried the man-cub.

"That's my boy!" chortled Baloo. "And you're going to make one swell bear. Why, you can even sing like a bear!"

"Now, that's an outright lie!" thought Bagheera. "That puny man-cub sounds no more like a bear. . . ."

But Mowgli, greatly encouraged, was singing away merrily, caroling about the bare necessities of life and how they would come to him.

Then, quite without warning, the singing stopped, and Bagheera could hear shrieking and chattering in the treetops, whooping and howling that chilled his blood. It was the bandar-log—the monkey-people! And Baloo was shouting something about flat-nosed, little-eyed creeps!

"They've gotten Mowgli!" gasped Bagheera.

Quicker than thought, he was down from the tree and speeding along the stream bank.

"Let go of me!" shouted Mowgli from somewhere high above.

There were shrill peals of high-pitched laughter,

then Baloo cried, "Take your flea-picking hands off of my cub!"

The monkeys laughed even more wildly.

"Give me back my man-cub!" roared Baloo.

A rain of fruit, some of it very, very ripe, and some of it very, very hard, descended on Baloo. Raging, the bear crashed about, colliding with trees and tearing up bushes.

"Baloo!" screamed Mowgli. "Baloo! Help! Help me!"

Bagheera was in time to see Baloo stagger backward and roll down a small hill. The monkeys shouted a few choice insults at the bear, then sped off through the treetops, taking Mowgli with them. Bagheera had one horrifying glimpse of the man-cub being passed from one monkey to another as the troop of gibbering clowns fled. The imbeciles! They were holding the man-cub by the ankle!

"Bagheera!" bellowed Baloo. "Bagheera! Bagheera!"

The panther looked down the hill at the bear, who was wallowing to his feet and shouting. "Bagheera!" he cried again.

"I see that it's happened," said Bagheera nastily.

The bear looked up and blinked. "Oh," he said in what was for him a very soft, small voice. "You heard me, huh?"

"How did it happen?" asked Bagheera.

"They ambushed me!" Baloo clambered up the hill. "There were thousands of them. I jabbed with my left, and I swung with a right, and then I led—"

"For heaven's sake!" snapped the panther. "What happened?"

"Those mangy monkeys carried him off," said Baloo miserably.

"I saw that!" roared Bagheera. "But how? How could you let them? How did they. . . . Oh, never mind!"

Bagheera turned his eyes toward the treetops. No use trying to follow that way. The bandar-log could travel like the wind through the upper roads of the jungle, through branches so high and thin that they would snap and break beneath the weight of a panther.

"We'd best get started," Bagheera announced briskly. "It will be night before we can reach the ancient ruins."

"The old temple?" Baloo said, wondering. "The man-place?"

"There are no men there now," Bagheera pointed out. "There are only the bandar-log and that lunatic king of theirs. That's where they'll take the man-cub —to their king!"

"But . . . but Bagheera," protested Baloo, "none of us ever go to the man-place!"

"Well, we're going now," insisted Bagheera. "And we'd better hurry, or we just might be too late."

The panther waited for no more discussion. Without even glancing again at Baloo, he turned and disappeared into the jungle.

"But we never go to the man-place!" said Baloo again. Then he sighed, shrugged, and lumbered after Bagheera. He was not singing now, and he moved with amazing speed.

6.

The Monkey King

Mowgli soon stopped shouting. It did no good. It only made the monkeys laugh. Besides, when he swung upside down a hundred feet above the ground he had no breath for cries. And for a good portion of the time Mowgli was upside down. The monkeys passed him from hand to hairy hand, clutching at his wrists, his ankles, seizing a knee or an elbow as the opportunity offered. Once one of them let him fall, and the man-cub saw the earth hurtling up at him and drew in his breath, ready to die. But quick little hands caught him, tossing him to be snatched and thrown again.

The monkeys howled with glee.

Mowgli turned, falling free, seeing earth, then sky, then earth again. Again the dark, strong hands snatched and caught, and again came the horrid, shrill laughter.

Another game, Mowgli thought wretchedly. But this was not like the wolves' games, or like funny old Baloo playing on the stream bank. The monkeys were playing with him as he and his brothers would play with a stick: toss and catch, race and run, and toss again.

It went on and on. Sometimes they were high, high in the trees, with Mowgli's stomach lurching toward his breastbone. Sometimes they raced through the lower branches, dodging and twisting to avoid hanging vines. Sometimes Mowgli's eyes blurred and his sight dimmed and he did not know where he was. Once he thought he heard Raksha speaking to him. "You must have nothing to do with the bandar-log," she seemed to say. "They are mad, thoroughly mad, and completely unreliable!"

"But I didn't have anything to do with them!" cried

Mowgli. "They came to me!"

The hideous laughter rang all around him and he started awake again. Raksha was not there. Instead there were the faces—the leering, laughing, hairy little faces—and the long arms pointing at something.

What was it? Stones were heaped upon stones to make strange shapes. Stones had fallen upon stones to make jagged, jumbled heaps. Mowgli drew in his breath sharply. The man-place! His mother had told him of it once when he nestled close to her in the warm safety of their den. She had said that long, long ago men had come to the place and piled their stones high to make walls and towers. They had roofed their walls over to shut out the jungle, and they called the place their temple. They had lived for a long time in the temple, going about their affairs with much bustle and importance. Always the jungle had waited, peeping over the walls, prying with soft green fingers at the chinks between the stone.

Then one day, for some reason which everyone had forgotten, the men had gone away. They had gone very suddenly, taking nothing with them. The little green fingers of the jungle had pulled at the walls then and tugged at the roofs. Vines had tumbled the stones

down, and mosses had slimed the paving of the court-
yards. But still the scent of man lingered. It was always
there, faint beneath the scent of the jungle.

"It is not a good place," the Mother Wolf had
warned. "It is a man-place, and we never go there. No
one goes there but the lizards who scuttle under the
rocks, and the monkey king."

Mowgli thought now that he should have asked his
mother on that warm, safe night why the monkey
king chose to live in the man-place. But Mowgli had
been sleepy—warm and safe and sleepy. And now he
was not warm or safe, and he would soon learn the
reason.

The monkeys scaled the wall easily, carrying Mowgli between them. "We have him! We have him!"
they shrieked. "Here he is! We have him!" And they
grasped Mowgli by his ankles and lowered him inside
the wall.

Even upside down, Mowgli knew that he was looking at the monkey king. The big beast was much larger
than any of his swarms of subjects, and much, much
uglier. His face was creased in a thousand folds, and
his reddish-brown pelt was thick and long. He lolled
back on a great stone chair which was carved with the

faces of weird, impossible creatures—creatures unlike anything Mowgli had ever seen. The monarch was noisily devouring a banana, and had obviously disposed of the peel by putting it on top of his head.

"Ha-ha-ha!" chuckled the king, without bothering to swallow his banana. "So this is the man-cub?"

Heaped at the foot of the stone chair were jewels—diamonds, emeralds, rubies, and pearls. Once, no doubt, they had been treasured by the men who had walked in this courtyard. Mowgli had heard it told that men love to decorate themselves with bright bits of glittering stone. It was said that they set great store on such things. Now, as Mowgli watched, the monkey king reached to pick up a gem that flashed bloodred fire in the waning light. The king put the gem to his eye, squinting, and peered through it at the boy. "Sooo!" he said. "Crazy!"

Mowgli did not like his position. The longer he stayed there dangling by his heels the more his face felt flushed and swollen and the harder the blood pounded in his ears. He was afraid that he would faint again. "I'm not crazy!" he shouted. "I'm not nearly as crazy as you are! Put me down!"

The monkeys who were holding him let go, and he

thudded to the stone floor of the courtyard with a jolt that knocked the breath from his body. It took him a little time to recover, but the instant he could he jumped to his feet and cried, "You cut that out!"

The king's hairy hand fastened on Mowgli's breech-cloth, and the boy felt himself lifted into the air. "Cool it, man-cub!" warned the king, not too unkindly. "Unwind yourself." Mowgli, struggling, suddenly found that the king was shaking his hand.

"Come on, cousin," coaxed the ape. "Shake."

Mowgli snatched his hand away. The king, undisturbed, put out a hairy foot, as if Mowgli might prefer to shake that instead.

"I am not your cousin," protested Mowgli.

"Of course you're my cousin," said the king evenly. "You're a man-cub, aren't you? You walk on your hind legs, don't you? Well, so do I, cousin." The king took a brief stroll around his throne to demonstrate.

"You've got a thumb that turns in, and so do I." His Majesty flexed his hands before Mowgli's eyes.

"I may have a little more hair than you do," admitted the king, glancing down at himself, "but that's just an incidental. We're cousins, cousin!"

Mowgli shuddered. Could it be true? "Wha—what

do you want me for?" he asked, trying to keep the quaver out of his voice.

The king grinned and slumped back on his throne. "Well, now," he began, "word has reached my royal ear that you want to stay in the jungle. Have a banana?"

Mowgli suddenly remembered his mother saying, "The monkey-people listen to everything. They carry tales. Never trust them." But he put the thought of Raksha out of his mind. The wolves had cast him out. He must get help wherever he could. He took the banana.

"Your good old cousin can fix it for you," promised the king. "Have two bananas."

Mowgli didn't really want two, but there seemed no way to refuse, especially when the monkey king popped the bananas neatly out of their skins and into the boy's mouth.

"Have we got a deal?" asked the king.

Mowgli couldn't answer right away. He was struggling with his bananas.

"Well?" said the king.

Mowgli gulped. "I'll do anything to stay in the jungle," he declared.

"Anything?" asked the king. There came an odd little glitter in his eyes, and Mowgli thought nervously that he was indeed mad. Perhaps the man-cub could turn now and run. But a glance showed him that this was impossible. All about, silent in the dusk, were the monkey king's subjects, hundreds upon hundreds of them, perched on the walls, skulking in the shadows of the courtyard, ringing the throne.

Mowgli nodded in agreement. "Anything," he said resignedly.

"Well, then," said the king, "I'll lay it on the line for you. I want to be a man, man-cub!"

Mowgli stared, hardly able to believe his ears. So that was it! That was why the monkey king chose to live in the man-place! He wanted to be a man! That's what he was playing at, sitting in the big stone chair that men had carved, running his hands through the heaps of glistening stones that men had left behind. He was playing at being a man!

His Majesty stood up, scratched himself briefly under the ribs, then reached a long arm to the vine that hung across the courtyard.

"I'm the king of the swingers!"

he crooned. He pulled himself up onto the vine and made his way swiftly, using hands and feet, to the top of the wall.

"I'm the jungle VIP,"

sang the king.

> "I've reached the top
> And had to stop,
> And that's what's bothering me.
> I want to be a man, man-cub,
> And stroll right into town,
> And be just like the other men.
> I'm tired of monkeying 'round!"

The king swung down again, grasped Mowgli's hands, and twirled the boy around.

"Oooh-be-doo!"

warbled the ape.

"I want to be like you-hoooo!"

Behind Mowgli, the monkeys began their own chorus of "hoop-do-heeps," keeping time to His Majesty's song.

94

"I want to walk like you,
  Talk like you, too.
  You see it's true,
  An ape like me
  Can learn to be
  A human, too!"

The king finished, standing triumphantly atop his throne. In spite of himself, Mowgli laughed. Then, so that His Majesty would take no offense, he said hastily, "Gee, cousin, you're real good!"

The king grinned a satisfied grin. He had always believed firmly in his own excellence, but it was nice to have his opinion confirmed by an appreciative cousin. "Now," he said, settling down to business, "here's your part of the deal. Lay the secret on me of man's red flower!"

"Red flower?" said Mowgli. "Fire? But I don't know how to make fire!"

The king's smile vanished, and his muddy eyes were suddenly streaked with red. His long fingers tangled in Mowgli's hair and pulled tight.

"Ouch!" cried the boy.

"You're a man, aren't you, man-cub?" snarled the

monkey king. "Of course you know how to make fire. Don't try to kid me!"

Mowgli had just begun to feel a bit comfortable in the company of the king. Now his heart leaped up to his throat. What would the monkey king do to him? How could he convince him that he did not have the secret of the red flower?

But then the king's grasp on the man-cub's hair loosened. His Majesty patted Mowgli's head. "I made a deal with you," he said very softly. "The red flower, that's all I need. Come on, man-cub, give me the secret."

Mowgli tried desperately to think of the right words. How could he explain it? But the monkey king's attention had strayed from the man-cub. Lost in some glorious vision that existed only inside his twisted brain, the king began to croon again:

> "I want to be a man, man-cub.
> I made a deal with you.
> What I desire is man's red fire
> To make my dream come true!"

All around Mowgli the monkey king's subjects stirred and shifted, weaving and swaying, their little hands clapping time, their feet beating on the stones that paved the courtyard. It was infectious. Almost against his will Mowgli found himself swaying, too, and then singing along with the bandar-log in their chant to the king's impossible dream.

7.
The Rescue

THE SUN had gone down before Bagheera and Baloo reached the temple. Even the red glow in the western sky had faded. The moon had not yet risen, and the narrow paths that twisted beneath the trees were inky black. Neither Bagheera nor Baloo cared. They knew darkness as well as they knew light, and it hindered them not at all.

"We must be careful," warned Bagheera. He stared up at the vine-covered walls that marked the monkey king's domain. "There may be lookouts posted."

"I'll clobber them!" muttered Baloo. He always liked direct action.

"Oh, fine!" said Bagheera. "Make a row. Raise the alarm. That way we'll never get the man-cub back!"

Baloo subsided, grumbling softly, and the two began a slow circuit of the crumbling walls.

There was no lookout. The monkey king, dreaming his vain dreams of manhood, had not bothered to order any of his subjects to keep watch atop the walls, and the featherbrained horde who waited upon His Majesty were incapable of that much forethought. Besides, why crouch atop a wall when one could crowd close into the courtyard and watch the man-cub? So it was that none saw the two shadows move beyond the walls, or noticed when the bear and the panther came to the place where the jungle had hurled down the stones.

Baloo and Bagheera looked in. There was Mowgli, to all appearances safe and sound. There was the monkey king crouched on his throne. There were the king's tribe, monkeys by the hundreds, all staring at Mowgli and the king, and yet not still. They were shuffling, dancing in lines, swaying to and fro, and beating time with their fists on stones, on each other, on themselves. The king himself swayed, singing. "Give me the power of man's red flower," he chanted, "so I can be like you!"

"Red flower!" gasped Bagheera. "Fire! So that's what that scoundrel is after!"

"I'll tear him limb from limb!" growled Baloo.

"Oh, be quiet!" snapped Bagheera. "This will take brains, not brawn."

"You'd better believe it," agreed Baloo, "and I'm loaded with both!"

Bagheera had no very high opinion of Baloo's brain-power, and it made him distinctly uneasy to see that the bear was clapping, very, very softly, in time to the music of the monkeys, and that Baloo's feet moved in an intricate little dance.

"Will you listen?" demanded Bagheera.

"Oh, yeah, yeah!" breathed Baloo. He was clapping a bit louder now, and his feet moved more joyfully. "Man, what a beat!" he exclaimed.

Bagheera tried to ignore this. "I have a plan," he said. His voice had taken on a sharp edge. "You must create a disturbance!"

"Yeah, man!" Baloo grinned. He was good at that sort of thing.

"While the monkeys are watching you," explained Bagheera, "I will dash in and get Mowgli away."

Baloo said nothing. He danced, his eyes shut and his well-rounded hindquarters switching in time to the monkey king's song.

"Got that?" asked Bagheera.

Baloo danced on.

"I said, have you got that?" demanded Bagheera.

"I'm gone, man," said Baloo. "Solid gone!"

And in an instant he was indeed gone. "Oh, no!" groaned Bagheera, who could hear him twitching and dancing his way through the darkness. Stones rolled and scattered as Baloo, hurrying to be in the center of things, scrambled through the breach in the wall and joined the outermost circle of gyrating, chanting monkeys.

"I wanted a disturbance," said Bagheera to himself, "but this is too much."

The monkeys, however, were far too absorbed in their revels to notice the arrival of the newcomer. They whirled and stamped, sang and whined through their noses, clapped their hands, and beat on the great stone columns that still stood firm, holding the remnants of the temple roof toward the sky. Even when Baloo

danced through the throng to the center of the courtyard and reeled wildly in front of the king, no one
raised an outcry. They thought, if they could be
accused of thinking at all, that this was just another
monkey—a very large, shaggy monkey.

"Madness," thought Bagheera. "Absolute madness!"

The panther glided over the stones and into the
shadows beneath the temple walls. He made no sound,
not that this mattered at all. No one was listening or
watching. All, even Mowgli, were caught up in the
frenzy of the dance.

A panther carved from stone sat in a niche in the
temple wall. Bagheera slipped quickly into the empty
niche next to the stone cat, bared his teeth in imitation
of the petrified one's snarl, and watched.

"I want to be like you-hoo-hoo!"

the king sang.

"I want to walk like you,
Talk like you, too-hoo-hoo!
You see it's true-hoo-hoo!
Someone like me-hee-hee
Can learn to be-hee-hee
Just like someone like you!"

Bagheera was distressed to note that Mowgli seemed delighted to be the object of so much admiration. Raksha could not have taught her cub to be careful in choosing his friends.

"I'll ape your mannerisms,"

promised the king.

"We'll be a set of twins.
No one will know where the man-cub ends
And the monkey king begins!"

"Revolting idea!" said Bagheera to himself.

"And when I eat bananas
I won't peel them with my feet,
'Cause I'm going to be a man, man-cub,
And learn some. . . ."

What the monkey king was going to learn Bagheera would never know, for at that instant Baloo broke in with an irrepressible "Doo-be-doo-be!" and whirled just a shade too near His Majesty.

"What?" cried the monarch. "Who?"

The king recognized that this was a very large monkey. Very large indeed. Too big for an ape, really. More like a—more like a bear!

"Baloo!" shouted the king. "It's Baloo the bear!"

The singing and the dancing stopped abruptly.

"Uh-oh!" said Baloo.

"Baloo!" The cry went up from the monkeys. "Baloo the bear!"

"That's him!"

"Yeah! That's him!"

"How'd he get in here?"

"Get him!"

Baloo was not generally noted for quick thinking, but he knew exactly what to do when, seeking to rescue a man-cub, a bear is menaced by hundreds of monkeys and one large, outraged monkey king. The proper procedure, Baloo was sure, was to pick up the man-cub, tuck him firmly under one arm, and run like mad. This Baloo did.

He ran in the wrong direction, of course. There simply wasn't time to plot a course. His first frantic dash did not take him to the breach in the wall. It took him into the interior of the old temple.

It was dark—much darker than the courtyard, where at least the stars cast a faint glow. And Baloo did not know the curving, twisting corridors. Dozens of little hands and feet fastened upon him, clutching at his fur, his head, his ears, covering his eyes. Still he ran on, holding fast to his man-cub, who was too startled even to cry out.

It was the collision with the temple gong that did it at last. Baloo crashed into the great bronze disk in the darkness. He thought he was going deaf as his head swelled with the ringing. His grip loosened for a moment. With a low chuckle, the monkey king seized Mowgli, turned, and ran.

But at the first bend in the corridor the king screamed suddenly and reversed direction. Bagheera barred the way, muscles tensed to spring, fangs bared. The monkey king fled down the winding ways of the temple, always clutching the boy. Behind him came the panther, more terrible than any night.

It is likely that Bagheera would have settled the matter then and there had not five very young, very imprudent monkeys leaped down from the columns and seized him by the tail. They were hardly a danger to the panther, but they were an annoyance, and it took several moments to send them scampering and squealing toward the courtyard. It took several moments, and it cost Bagheera a bite on the ear. And when he turned about, the monkey king and Mowgli were nowhere to be seen.

A scream came from the heart of the temple, and Bagheera grinned in satisfaction. The ape had met again with Baloo, and it sounded as if the tough old bear was giving a good account of himself. Bagheera sped toward the noise.

But now the monkeys, screeching frantically in the courtyard, had evolved a battle plan of sorts. They came in, in a great, black, howling horde, thirsting for blood.

Bagheera burst into the central room of the temple to see the monkey king holding Mowgli fast under one long arm and speeding around and around a stone column. Baloo, reaching vainly for the boy, raced close behind.

"We've got to get out!" cried Bagheera. "The monkeys! They're all coming together!"

Baloo caught at the column to stop himself. A huge piece of masonry slipped loose and came away in his hand. There was an ominous rumble from somewhere high overhead.

"Get the man-cub!" shouted Bagheera. "Run!"

The monkey king stopped dead and looked up,

listening. A small piece of stone fell from the ceiling and struck him on the nose.

"The roof!" he squealed. "My roof! My beautiful roof!"

And he abandoned the man-cub, dumping Mowgli down on the floor and running for dear life.

Bagheera streaked in, seized Mowgli by his breech-cloth, and ran. Baloo, finally comprehending the situation, ran after him.

They battered their way out, wading through successive waves of monkeys. The hordes in the back pressed forward crying, "Get them! Get them!" The ones in front, hearing the threatening rumble overhead, reversed directions and pressed back against the advancing monkeys, crying, "Out! Out of the way! Let me out!"

Bagheera and Baloo gained the open court as stones began to fall. One large block of limestone caught Bagheera's tail, but the panther pulled himself free and ran on, holding grimly to Mowgli. Baloo was pelted from above and behind, but he staggered on. Behind them the rescuers could hear the sliding crash of falling masonry and the shrieks of the monkeys fleeing from their man-place. The bear and the panther did not look back, and now Mowgli struggled free of Bagheera's grip and he, too, ran. They sped through the night, through the ruined wall and into the shelter of the friendly jungle. Only when the crashing and the cries of the monkeys had faded to silence did they stop to look around and catch their breaths.

"Good heavens!" panted Bagheera.

"Yeah, man!" Baloo agreed.

"What . . . what happened?" asked the dazed Mowgli.

"I imagine it was Baloo," speculated Bagheera. "He pulled a stone loose from a column, and the whole wretched place began coming down."

"Man!" said Baloo again. And then he chuckled a deep, happy chuckle. "It was a real swinging party!" said Baloo the bear.

8.

Baloo's
Sacrifice

Mowgli slept that night beneath a great banyan tree far from the shattered temple of the monkey king. Baloo slept, too, deeply as always, snoring from time to time and smiling as he dreamed of combs dripping with honey and fruit ripening on the trees. Only Bagheera remained awake to keep watch through the night.

Once the panther heard the army of the monkey king screaming and chattering in the trees. But they were far away to the south, doubtless searching through the upper terraces of the jungle for the escaped man-cub. Bagheera smiled his contempt. It would never occur to the idiot monkeys to come to the ground, where they might reasonably expect to find the trail of their quarry. No, they would rush back and forth through the trees, screeching mindlessly at one another, and by morning most of them would forget what it was they were searching for.

But Bagheera did not dismiss the monkey king's subjects entirely from his mind. Sooner or later, if Mowgli remained in the jungle, the monkeys would come upon him again. It would happen by chance, but it would happen. And what then?

The sky in the east paled and went gray, and the stars dimmed. Soon it would be morning. Bagheera touched Baloo gently on the shoulder.

The bear did not stir.

Bagheera prodded again, not so gently this time.

Baloo rolled over and opened one eye. "Huh?" said he.

"Get up," whispered the panther. "I want to talk with you."

"Aw, Baggy!" protested the bear. "Not again! Besides, it's still dark."

"Get up!" insisted Bagheera. "It's important."

"Oh, sure, sure!" grumbled Baloo. "It's always important." But he heaved himself to his feet and began to rub the sleep out of his eyes, yawning mightily.

Bagheera waited a moment, wanting to choose his words with care. Then, since Baloo showed signs of dozing off again, he began. "I am sure you have noticed, Baloo, that Mowgli has man's ability to get into trouble."

Baloo nodded drowsily. "Little Britches is a real smart kid," he agreed.

This was not quite the idea Bagheera had intended to convey, but the panther fought down his irritation and went on as evenly as possible. "Your influence," he accused, "has not been exactly what—"

"Shh!" interrupted Baloo.

"I beg your pardon," said Bagheera, "but I must—"

"Keep it down," Baloo said. "You're going to wake up the kid. He's had a big day."

"Indeed he has," was Bagheera's wry comment.

"A real sockeroo!" said Baloo admiringly. "You know, Baggy, it isn't easy learning to be like me!"

"Let's be thankful for small favors," snapped Bagheera. "But he did pretty well. What a disgraceful performance, associating with those undesirable, scatterbrained monkeys!"

Baloo ignored Bagheera. He thought Mowgli looked cold, curled up there with his head pillowed on the roots of the banyan tree. Carefully the bear pulled up a handful of ferns and tucked them over the sleeping man-cub.

"I hope that Mowgli has learned something from his experience," said Bagheera.

Mowgli smiled and mumbled something in his sleep. To the panther's outraged ears it sounded very much like, "I want to be like you-hoo-hoo!"

"That's my boy!" chuckled Baloo.

"Nonsense!" said Bagheera. Then, desperately, he went on. "Baloo, I must have a word with you!"

"A word?" Baloo looked around at the panther. It seemed to him that Bagheera had already had a word —a number of words—in fact, far too many words, considering the hour. Didn't the dratted panther ever sleep? "You mean you want to talk *some more?*" asked the bear.

"Over here, please." Bagheera nodded toward the pool that lay just beyond the spread of the banyan tree.

"Oh, all right." Baloo did not feel up to an argument.

Not before dawn, at any rate. He shambled along behind the panther until they came to the edge of the pool. Then, so that the trip would not be an utter waste, he bent and took a drink of water.

Bagheera got briskly to the point. "Baloo," he said, "the man-cub must go back to the man-village. The jungle is not the place for him."

Baloo had heard all this before, and it was not of the slightest interest to him. He looked about for breakfast and spotted some berries hanging from a bramble which had crept up a nearby tree. He helped himself to a handful of berries and began to eat them slowly, one at a time. They were a bit tart, but not really sour. "I grew up in the jungle," said the bear, "and take a look at me."

"Yes, indeed," said Bagheera. "Just take a look at yourself."

Baloo leaned over to peer into the pool.

"Look at that eye!" commanded Bagheera.

Baloo grinned. His left eye was swollen almost completely shut. Perhaps it had been the collision with the temple gong that had done it, or perhaps it had been the clutching hands of the monkey king. Baloo didn't know and didn't care. It was a magnificent shiner, an honorable mark of courage. "It's beautiful, isn't it?" the bear gurgled happily.

"Ugh!" said Bagheera. "Frankly, you're a disreputable sight!"

Baloo resented this. It was just too bad if a bear couldn't get into a little scuffle once in a while. He turned and glared at Bagheera. "Well," he remarked, "you don't look exactly like a basket of fruit yourself."

This was true enough. The monkeys had left their marks on Bagheera's sleek hide, and the tip of the panther's right ear showed signs of having been chewed briefly. Bagheera quickly abandoned appearance as a subject of conversation and returned to the main attack.

"Baloo, you cannot adopt Mowgli as your son," he said firmly.

"Why not?" demanded the bear.

The panther hesitated. How could he get through to this silly bear just how idiotic the idea was? Baloo waited, calmly munching on his berries.

"Birds of a feather should flock together," said Bagheera at last.

Baloo nodded. That was reasonable enough.

"Like seeks like," said Bagheera.

Baloo nodded again, still eating, and Bagheera knew that he had not reached the bear—not at all.

"Let me put it this way," said Bagheera. "You wouldn't marry a panther, would you?"

Baloo gave the question due consideration. Then he began to laugh softly. "I don't know," he replied. "Come to think of it, no panther ever asked me." And he went off into gales of laughter, rolling over and over on the ground.

"Baloo!" cried Bagheera.

Baloo stopped laughing and sat up, wiping his eyes. "You've got to be serious about this!" insisted Bagheera. "The man-cub is not a bear. He is a man-cub. Someday he will be a man, and then. . . ."

Baloo sighed. Bagheera was tiresome, always worrying about what might happen someday. If he'd only stop talking so much and relax a little! The bear backed up to a tree and idly began scratching his shoulder blades. "Stop worrying, Baggy," he counseled. "I'll take care of Little Britches, and—"

Bagheera had been expecting Baloo to say this. He was more than ready for it. "Of course you'll take care of him," he said coldly. "Just as you took care of him when the monkeys kidnapped him, eh?"

Baloo continued his scratching. "Aw," he mumbled, "can't a guy make one mistake?"

"Not in the jungle!" said Bagheera.

It was true. Baloo knew it.

"Another thing"—Bagheera pressed the attack while he still had the upper hand—"sooner or later Mowgli will meet Shere Khan!"

Baloo stopped scratching and became very, very attentive.

"Shere Khan?" he asked.

Bagheera nodded.

"The tiger?" questioned Baloo again.

Again Bagheera nodded.

"Old Stripes?" said Baloo, hoping against hope that he might have mistaken Bagheera's meaning.

But again Bagheera nodded.

"But what's Shere Khan got against the kid?" asked Baloo. "I know he's pretty mean, even for a tiger, but why should Mowgli be his particular dish of cat food?"

"He hates man with a vengeance. You know that," Bagheera pointed out. "He fears man's gun and man's fire."

"But Little Britches hasn't any gun," protested

Baloo. "And he can't make fire!"

"And Shere Khan won't wait until he can," Bagheera said. "He'll get Mowgli while he's young and helpless. Just one swipe. . . ."

Bagheera unsheathed his claws and swept the air under Baloo's nose. The bear drew back, shuddering. "No!" he cried.

"Yes," insisted Bagheera.

"No!" snarled Baloo. "No!"

Bagheera did not answer. He had won and he knew it.

"Well," began Baloo, "what are we going to do?"

"We'll do what's best for the man-cub," said the panther quietly.

"You'd better believe it!" cried Baloo. "You'd better believe it. You just name it and I'll do it!"

"Good!" said the panther. "Then you'll make Mowgli go to the man-village."

"What?" shouted Baloo. "Are you out of your mind?"

Bagheera kept still and let the bear storm on.

"I promised him he could stay in the jungle with me!" cried Baloo.

"That's just the point," said Bagheera relentlessly.

118

"As long as he does remain here with you, he's in danger. It's up to you."

"Up to me?" Baloo didn't like this at all. "You mean . . . you mean I've got to tell him?"

Bagheera nodded.

"But why me?" asked the wretched bear.

"Because he won't listen to me," said Bagheera.

"But . . . but I love that kid like he was my own cub," mourned Baloo.

"That's very nice, I'm sure," said Bagheera. "No doubt it would be great fun to have your man-cub with you. But do you love him enough to do what's best for him? Do you love him enough to make the sacrifice and take him to his own people?"

Baloo slumped, utterly defeated. "Can't I wait until morning?" he asked.

Bagheera looked to the east. The sky was pink. The sun was just below the horizon. "Think of what's best for Mowgli," he warned. "Don't think of yourself."

Baloo nodded miserably.

"Then," said Bagheera, very gently, "do what you must. It's morning now. Go on, Baloo."

The bear gulped. Then he went very, very slowly back to the banyan tree and the sleeping man-cub.

Bagheera stayed at the pool.

"Mowgli," said Baloo. "Mowgli, it's time to get up."

Mowgli smiled as he wakened, stretching and blinking up at Baloo. "Oh, hi," he said happily. "Hi, Baloo!"

Baloo grinned a sickly grin. "Hey, rub that old sleep out of your eyes, Little Britches," he said, attempting to sound like his usual hearty self. "You and I have a long walk ahead of us."

"Swell!" Mowgli obediently rubbed his eyes. "We'll have lots of fun together." The boy sat up and pushed the ferns aside.

"Sure," said Baloo. "Yeah! All right." Then, after a brief pause, he added, "Let's hit the trail, kid."

The bear turned to Bagheera, who was sitting quietly near the pool. "See you around, Bagheera," he said.

Mowgli skipped behind Baloo in great good spirits. "Good-bye, Bagheera," he called. "Baloo and I have things to do."

"Good-bye, man-cub," said Bagheera, "and good luck."

If there was a note of sadness in the farewell, Mowgli did not notice it. He hurried on, passing Baloo, crying joyfully, "Come on! All we have to do is look for the bare necessities!"

"Yeah!" said Baloo. "Sure. You bet, Mowgli."

Mowgli began to sing, dancing along under the trees, and the song was Baloo's.

"The bare necessities,"

warbled the man-cub.

"The simple bare necessities!
Forget about your worries and your strife!"

"Yeah!" mumbled Baloo. "You know it." And the discouraged bear sat down abruptly on a stone.

Mowgli, having learned his lessons from Baloo very well indeed, bumped into a slender banana tree and brought a single banana tumbling down.

"I mean the bare necessities,"

he caroled.

"That's why a bear can rest at ease,
With just the bare necessities of life!"

He courteously handed the banana to Baloo. "I'll live here in the jungle all my life!" he declared happily as he went to the tree for another banana. "I like being a bear."

He began to eat, then noticed that Baloo did not seem to be hungry. The bear was sitting and staring at his banana as if he had never seen one before and wasn't quite sure what to do with it.

"Where are we going, Baloo?" Mowgli asked.

"Well," said Baloo, "it's . . . uh . . . well, it's sort of new and different, and . . . uh. . . ." Baloo's voice trailed off into nothing.

"I don't care," said Mowgli. "I don't care where we go, as long as I'm with you." He took Baloo's great paw in both his hands and squeezed it.

Baloo found this very upsetting. He drew his paw away abruptly, cleared his throat, and said, "Mowgli, look, there's something I've got to tell you."

"Okay, Baloo." Mowgli was ready enough to listen. But a butterfly fluttered past and Mowgli, light-headed as any monkey, jumped up and ran after it.

Baloo drew a deep breath. "Gee whiz," he rumbled. "Now, how did old Baggy put it?"

"What's that, Baloo?" asked Mowgli. The butterfly lighted on a bush and Mowgli crept close to stare at the gaudy wings.

122

"Baggy said," began Baloo, " 'You wouldn't marry a panther, would you?' "

Mowgli laughed. What a silly question! "I don't know what you're talking about," he told Baloo.

Baloo tried again. "Mowgli, don't you realize that you're a human?"

"Not anymore, Baloo. I'm a bear now, like you." To prove it, Mowgli bared his teeth and growled as ferociously as possible. The butterfly flitted off.

"Little Britches, listen to me," pleaded Baloo.

"Grrr!" growled Mowgli. He raised his arms and danced, dodging and twisting like a very small, skinny fighting bear. "Come on, Baloo!" he laughed. "Circle and weave!" Mowgli jumped to punch Baloo's midsection, then stood back and waited confidently for the bear to return the attack. Instead Baloo reached out, grasped Mowgli's wrists firmly, and held the boy still.

"Now, stop it!" commanded Baloo. "Hold still. I want to tell you something."

Mowgli giggled. Baloo looked so funny when he was being serious. "What's the matter, old papa bear?" asked the man-cub teasingly.

"Look, Mowgli," Baloo said, "I've been trying to

123

tell you . . . I've been trying since you woke up. I've got to take you back to the man-village!"

Mowgli's giggle faded.

"There!" said Baloo to himself. "It's done!"

Mowgli pulled away, horror-struck. "The man-village?" he echoed.

"Look, kid," said Baloo, "I can explain. Now, like Bagheera says—"

"You said we were partners!" shouted Mowgli.

"Believe me—" begged the bear.

"You're just like Bagheera!" Mowgli said accusingly.

"Just a paw-picking minute!" cried Baloo. "That's going too far!"

Mowgli turned and began to stamp away.

"Mowgli!" Baloo shouted. "Stop! Come back!"

Mowgli didn't even look around. He plunged into a bank of undergrowth and disappeared.

"Wait!" The bear crashed into the bushes. "Little Britches! Wait! Listen to old Baloo!"

The man-cub was gone.

"Mowgli?" called Baloo.

There was no sound.

"Mowgli!" The bear was shouting very loudly now.

Still no one answered.

"Mowgli? Little Britches! Answer me!"

The only reply to Baloo's cries was the appearance of Bagheera. The black panther materialized suddenly at the bear's side. *"Now* what happened?" he asked sourly.

The crestfallen Baloo looked down at the panther. "You're not going to believe this," he said sadly, "but I used the same words you did, and Mowgli ran out on me!"

Bagheera closed his eyes for a moment as if his head hurt him rather badly. "I believe it," he said.

"I goofed, huh?" asked Baloo.

The panther confirmed it. "You goofed."

The two stayed where they were for a time, Baloo awash with guilt and fear for Mowgli, Bagheera trying to fight down his anger at the bear's clumsiness. Then Bagheera remembered Mother Wolf and his promise that he would keep her cub safe. He remembered Kaa the python, perhaps waiting somewhere above a jungle trail, and the minions of the monkey king swarming through the trees. It was not a time for anger or faultfinding.

"Come on," said the panther. "Don't just stand there

worrying about it. We've got to find the man-cub."

And, nose to the ground, the panther started off on the search. After a moment's thought, Baloo followed him.

9.

The Search

Mowgli's trail would have been easy to follow even had Bagheera's nose not been so keen. It was plain to both the bear and the panther that the boy had run blindly through the jungle. No doubt, thought Bagheera, he was in a panic lest they overtake him and force him back to the man-village. The panther felt a surge of remorse at the sight of the torn vines and broken branches that marked the man-cub's progress. Once the boy had crossed a jungle trail. Instead of turning and following this easier path he had plunged

127

straight on into the dense undergrowth on the other side.

"We'd better find him soon," Baloo worried. "He'll tear himself apart if he keeps on like this."

Bagheera didn't answer, but he quickened his pace.

On and on went the track of the fleeing man-cub. Once, Bagheera noted, the boy had fallen and sprawled across the roots of a tree. Once he had slipped and tumbled down a muddy hill. And once he must have been frightened, for he had stopped for a time to hide under a bush.

When Baloo and Bagheera came to a river that rushed swiftly along under the trees, they saw that the man-cub had turned to run along the riverbank. The footprints showed clear and sharp in the soft loam beside the river. Mowgli had not traveled here with the tireless lope of the hunting wolf. He had raced like a driven deer, heels pounding down, each stride almost as long as himself.

"Poor kid!" mourned Baloo. "Poor Little Britches!"

"Save your breath!" snapped Bagheera. "If it hadn't been for you. . . ."

"But I only told him what you told me!" protested the bear.

Downstream, a huge tree had fallen across the river to make a broad bridge. The man-cub's trail went up over the roots of the tree and out across the trunk to the middle of the river. Then it vanished.

"He fell here," Bagheera announced. "He fell off!"

Baloo looked down at the water and then scanned each bank. "You don't suppose he . . . he. . . ."

"Drowned?" Bagheera finished the question for him. "Hardly. I daresay none of Raksha's cubs would ever drown. He'd come to one bank or the other farther downstream. We can pick up the trail there. But we've got to hurry. We've been too long on the way now. Shere Khan could be anywhere about, and if he finds the man-cub alone. . . ."

Bagheera made a raking motion with his claws. Baloo winced and shuddered.

"You take the left bank," Bagheera ordered, "and I'll take the right. If you find the place where he came out of the water, shout. I'll do the same. And hurry!"

Baloo did not need to be told twice. He was down off the fallen log in an instant and snuffling his way along the riverbank. Bagheera, for his part, took to the trees for a time. He knew the man-cub could not have gained dry ground until he was some distance below the log bridge. There was just an off chance that the panther could catch sight of the boy if he had a higher vantage point.

Neither Baloo nor Bagheera saw Kaa. The python had been curled around a tree limb almost directly over the fallen log. Listening to the bear and the panther talk, Kaa had felt a pang of bitter regret when he realized that the man-cub must have been there—right there—just beneath him. Mowgli had been within his reach, and he had not known. But the snake smiled his coldest smile at the thought that now the man-cub was alone. Kaa was not disposed at any time to hunt his prey. He preferred to let his victims come to him. But for Mowgli he was willing to make an exception. He uncoiled his sluggish length and let himself slip down, down past the log bridge, down into the water. The cool wetness was pleasant. It quieted the pain in his tail, which was still firmly knotted.

Kaa swam with the current. What better way to find the man-cub than to use the route which the man-cub had followed? Let old Baloo and that insolent panther sniff their slow way along the riverbank. Kaa would go as the man-cub had gone, and he would arrive before them.

Bagheera did not notice when the snake slid by. Kaa's head barely broke the surface of the water. Besides, Bagheera was not watching the river. He was peering at the jungle—that great stretch of green—green on green on green as far as the eye could see, with here and there a patch of blue where the sky showed through the trees, or a flash of brilliance when some bird flew.

Then the tree on which Bagheera stood began to shake, and to the panther's ears came the familiar command: "Hup . . . two . . . three . . . four! Keep it up . . . two . . . three . . . four!"

"Hathi!" exclaimed Bagheera.

Not long before, Bagheera had fondly hoped that he would not meet Hathi again for a long, long time. Now he was quite glad to see the pompous old bull elephant leading his herd along under the trees. Hathi might be somewhat ridiculous. Certainly he brooked no interference with his "military" affairs. But he was not vicious. And he was coming from downstream. Perhaps he had seen some sign of the man-cub.

"Company, sound off!" cried Hathi.

The elephants, marching in strict trunk-to-tail military formation, began to sing:

131

"Oh, we've marched from here to there,
And it doesn't matter where.
You can see us push
Through the deepest bush. . . ."

"Halt!" commanded Bagheera.

Hathi's troops were accustomed to obeying immediately and without question. They halted and stood
patiently, awaiting further orders.

"What?" roared Hathi. "Who? Who said that? I
give the commands here. Well? Well? Who was it?"

Bagheera came down from his tree. He didn't come
too quickly. It wouldn't do to give Hathi the impression that he was frightened. "I said that, Colonel," he
told Hathi.

"You, Bagheera?" Hathi could scarcely believe his
ears. Bagheera the panther, the cunning and courteous
one, giving orders to Hathi's troop? It could not be!

"What do you mean, sir?" Hathi demanded. "Do
you dare to take over my command?"

"Not at all, Colonel, not at all." Bagheera hastened
to placate the old elephant. "I'm terribly sorry to in-
terrupt your drilling. But I need your help."

"Highly irregular!" huffed Hathi. "We are on

132

important cross-country maneuvers!"

Hathi's little son ambled forward to lean comfortably against the leg of one of the sturdier cows in the troop. "What happened, Mama?" the young elephant wanted to know.

"Your father seems to have run into a roadblock," said the mother dryly.

"Another one?" asked the baby.

Fortunately Hathi did not hear. Or perhaps he only pretended not to hear. Quickly Bagheera explained his plight. "It's an emergency, Colonel," he told Hathi. "The man-cub is lost in the jungle. He ran away, and we must find him."

"Ran away?" rumbled Hathi. "Frightful! Terrible! Deserters everywhere. Don't know what the army's coming to these days!"

"No, no!" Bagheera protested. "He didn't run away from the army. He ran away from Baloo. Have you seen him?"

Hathi frowned. He disliked all this talk of runaways. It made for unrest in the ranks. He wished that Bagheera would leave so that he could get on with his maneuvers. A colonel had plenty to do, heaven knows, what with giving commands and inspecting and keeping his troops in order. No time to fret about runaways.

But Bagheera showed no signs at all of going away. "Seen who?" said Hathi at last.

"The man-cub!" Bagheera snapped. "Have you seen the man-cub?"

"Man-cub? Man-cub?" Hathi did recall having seen a man-cub not so very long ago. But where?

Bagheera snorted with exasperation. "The man-cub I was taking back to the man-village," he said. "Have you seen him?"

"Oh? Oh, *that* man-cub!" exclaimed Hathi, as if the jungle simply abounded with man-cubs. "Certainly I saw him. Yesterday, it was . . . or the day before. Trying to enlist in my troop. I told him then. . . ."

"No, no!" howled Bagheera. "Today! Today! Have you seen him today?" The panther stopped and tried to control himself. After a moment he went on, very carefully. "The man-cub is lost," he told Hathi. "He ran away."

"Disgraceful!" said Hathi. "Let me tell you, Bagheera, I give the orders here."

"Of course, Colonel Hathi, but. . . ."

"I told that man-cub to get out of the jungle," bellowed the elephant, his temper rising, "and when I give an order, I expect to be obeyed!"

"Naturally, Colonel," Bagheera agreed, "but the point is. . . ."

"What's the trouble?" muttered one of the elephants behind Hathi.

"Somebody's lost," answered another of the troops.

"Aren't we all?" muttered a third.

"The point is," Bagheera went on grimly, "that I have to find the man-cub. He's alone and helpless and in great danger. I just want to know, have you seen him?"

"The army has no time for lost civilians," harrumphed Hathi.

"Shere Khan may be near," Bagheera pleaded. "He hates the man-cub."

"Oh?" said Hathi. "I'm sorry." The old elephant really meant it. If Shere Khan had it in for the man-cub, that was pretty much that. Nothing anyone could do about it but be sorry. Besides, Hathi hadn't seen the man-cub. Not today. "Fortunes of war and all that sort of thing," he told Bagheera, as if that was any comfort.

"Now, just a minute!"

The cow elephant who had been stroking Hathi's

young son with her trunk put the baby away from her and came forward. "Now, just a minute!" she said again.

Hathi was aghast. "What are you doing out of ranks?" he demanded.

The mother elephant ignored the question. "How would you like to have *our* son alone and lost in the jungle?" she wanted to know.

Hathi looked at the baby, then quickly looked away.

"Of course you wouldn't," said the old bull's mate. "That little man-cub is no different from our son. We have to find him."

"But, my dear . . ." Hathi began to protest.

"We'll find him!" announced the mother elephant. "We'll find him, or I'll take over your command."

Had Hathi been capable of going pale, he would have done so. "What?" he cried. "Impossible! Against all tradition!"

"Tradition, my aching feet!" said his mate.

"Pop," put in the baby, "the man-cub's my friend!"

"Nonsense!" grumbled Hathi.

"If someone had just noticed some sign of him . . ." began Bagheera, trying desperately to keep the conversation on the track. But Hathi didn't hear. He was suddenly beguiled by a new idea. It was a brilliant idea. *He* would find the man-cub. He and his troops! Of course! What a splendid idea! And what an opportunity for special drill in searching techniques!

"Troopers!" thundered Hathi.

The herd snapped to attention.

"I need volunteers for a special assignment," said Hathi. "All of you will help find a lost man-cub."

"Interesting way to get volunteers," said Bagheera to himself.

"Sergeant!" Hathi was addressing a stout bull. "Take one squad and go to the east. I'll lead another squad on your left flank."

The sergeant saluted with his trunk.

"We'll keep three trunk-lengths apart," said Hathi. "That way there's no chance of his slipping past us. Remember, I expect everyone to do his duty!"

The mother elephant, well pleased with this development, took her place in her mate's squad and marched off.

Bagheera sighed as the troops moved out, a careful three trunk-lengths apart. "All I asked was whether they'd seen him," said the panther to himself, and he returned to the riverbank and patiently nosed along.

After he had gone for some distance without finding a trace of Mowgli, Bagheera plunged into the river and crossed over to the far bank. There were tracks there— Mowgli's small footprints, rather damp around the edges and obliterated in places by the gigantic tread of Baloo.

"I thought that nitwit bear was going to call me," muttered Bagheera. But then the panther thought of Hathi puffing and bellowing away. Even if Baloo had shouted, Bagheera would not have heard him.

Bagheera went on with his nose to the ground. The bear had not yet caught Mowgli, but he was close behind the man-cub. The scents of both were very fresh.

But something else had passed that way *after* the man-cub and the bear. There were marks on the ground—the marks of a serpent. "Kaa!" breathed Bagheera. He broke into a run. Before long he stopped, however, and laughed silently. The giant snake had somehow managed to get his knotted tail jammed between two stones. He was there beside the path, struggling to free himself.

"I s-s-say, my friend," he hissed when he saw Bagheera. "Would you mind giving me a hand here? It's rather difficult, you know, slithering with a knot."

"Another time, Kaa," Bagheera replied. "I can't stop now. I'm hunting a man-cub."

"S-S-So was I," said Kaa sadly.

"I know," said Bagheera, and he went on his way.

10.
The Vultures

AFTERWARD Mowgli always thought of it as "the dead place." The jungle ended there at the edge of a great plain, treeless and rock-studded, that stretched on and on until the sky bent to meet it. There was a pool. The man-cub, exhausted and trembling, came upon it when the sun was high and bent to drink. He drew back, however, his thirst forgotten, when he saw that the water was black as the wing of a raven. Beyond the pool, a dead and blasted tree struggled to keep a root-hold in the earth. On its scraggly, leafless limbs a company of huge birds clung like unwholesome fruit. Mowgli looked at them and shuddered. He had seen them before, or birds like them. They were the mur-dar-khor, the carrion eaters. They rode on the high winds scanning the jungle below for death. No wolf had to do with such as these—not while there was breath in him.

Mowgli looked past the vultures at the plain. It was endless. He could not go on that way. He would have to turn back into the jungle.

But the jungle meant Baloo, who had just betrayed him, and Bagheera, who would scold and lecture. There were others in the jungle whom he did not care to meet again. There was Kaa, the python. There was Hathi, the elephant of long memory and terrible temper. There was the monkey king, with his longing for the secret which Mowgli did not possess.

The man-cub could not go on across the plain. But how could he turn back into the jungle? Miserable, he sat down at the edge of the pool and peered at his own dark reflection.

"Hey, what are we going to do?" said someone behind Mowgli.

The man-cub looked around. One of the vultures

had spoken. It had to be a vulture. There was no one else in sight.

"Blimey, I don't know," said a second voice. "What do you want to do?"

"I've got it!" said a third vulture. "Let's flap over to the east side of the jungle. They've always got a bit of action—a bit of swinging scene!"

"Aw, come off it!" said another bird, and Mowgli recognized the voice of the first vulture who had spoken. "Things are right dead all over."

"You mean you wish they were!" howled another vulture, and he laughed so that the wrinkled red skin on his naked neck became almost purple.

Mowgli had an uneasy feeling that he had better go somewhere, either out across the plain or back into the jungle. Perhaps it didn't matter much which path he took, so long as he removed himself from the neighborhood of these strange birds.

"I say," said the first vulture, "what a crazy-looking bunch of bones!"

"Yeah! And sitting about by themselves!" said one of his fellows.

Mowgli realized that the birds had seen him. He was the crazy-looking bunch of bones. He would get up and

143

walk away slowly, to show he didn't care. He would pretend he hadn't heard at all.

But it was too late. "Let's have some fun with this little bloke!" suggested the first vulture, and in an instant the great birds had flapped up from their tree and were swooping toward Mowgli. If he went now he would have to run, and that he would not do. He turned back to the pool, picked up a bit of stick and began to stir the water idly, as if there were not a carrion bird within a thousand miles.

The man-cub was aware of the vultures alighting near him. He could hear the beating of their wings and the sound of claws scratching for a hold on the earth. He did not look up, not even when one of the great birds—the very largest one—sidled around in front of him and remarked, "Blimey! He's got legs like a stork, he has."

Mowgli fought down the impulse to pull his legs in under him. He went on quietly stirring the pond with his stick.

"He can't be a stork," said a second bird. "He ain't got no feathers, he ain't!" And the vulture leaned so close to Mowgli that his wing brushed the man-cub's arm.

144

Mowgli pulled away. "Leave me alone, you crazy birds!" he cried.

"Get *him!*" squawked one of the man-cub's tormentors. "He thinks *we're* crazy!"

This caused a general outburst of hilarity on the part of the vultures.

"I don't see what's so funny," said Mowgli.

"You will, mate," declared the largest of the birds. Slyly he nudged one of his companions. "You will when you meet old Gainda. He'll fracture you!"

The second vulture gleefully followed the big one's lead. "Ah, Gainda!" he croaked. "He's always good for a laugh. He'll knock you right out of your mind, he will."

Mowgli wasn't at all sure that he wanted to be knocked right out of his mind. Still, the way the vulture described it, the experience was great fun. Mowgli felt he could use a bit of fun just then. "Who's Gainda?" he asked.

"You'll find out!" said one of the birds.

Now, that did *not* sound like fun. It sounded almost like a threat.

"If you really want to know," said another vulture, a short and remarkably plump bird, "just climb up there and you'll see him." The feathered one extended his wing in the direction of a huge boulder which humped up above the grass of the plain.

"Go ahead!" urged the large vulture. "That is, unless you're afraid."

Mowgli was not afraid. Not exactly. But he was very uneasy. There was something about the way the vultures nudged one another and tittered behind their wings that set his scalp to prickling and sent a cold shiver down his spine. But, he reminded himself sternly, he was Raksha's cub. Besides, what harm could there be in climbing up on a rock?

"I am not afraid!" declared the man-cub. He jumped up and ran to clamber onto the boulder.

"Get him!" laughed one vulture.

"Aw, he is too afraid," taunted another.

"I'm not!" insisted Mowgli. "I'm not afraid."

The largest vulture, who seemed to be the ringleader of the group, hopped forward and looked up at Mowgli perched on the big stone. He put one wing to his head as if he had trouble hearing. "Say that again, just once more," he coaxed. "Say it so my little ear can hear it. But this time much louder! Say, 'I'm not afraid of Gainda!'"

146

Very loudly then, Mowgli shouted, "I'm not afraid of Gainda!"

And at that the world turned upside down. The sky hung for an instant at Mowgli's heels. There came a snorting and a bellowing, and the man-cub hit the earth with a sickening jolt. Then he found himself staring up past a wicked horn into a pair of dull, blinking little eyes.

A rhinoceros!

Of course it was a rhinoceros! Mowgli had heard of these big-horned, armor-plated earth-shakers. So that's who the vultures called Gainda! And they had tricked him into climbing right up on the beast's back.

Mowgli pulled himself away from the rhino, then scrambled to his feet and backed off.

"Who?" demanded the rhinoceros in a voice like falling stones. "Who said he ain't afraid?" The enormous head swung back and forth as the rhino tried in vain to focus on the wretch who had shouted the insult.

"Uh . . ." began Mowgli, who was now at a reasonably safe distance, ". . . er . . . I did . . . but. . . ."

The large vulture edged close to Mowgli and cackled, "Listen, new guy, new face on the scene,

Gainda ain't got all his marbles!"

The rhino heard it. But, then, the vulture had intended that he should. "I have too got all my marbles!" he roared.

"Besides," went on the vulture, his wicked little eyes sparking with mischief, "he's blind as a bat!"

"He can't see his ruddy horn in front of his face," confirmed another vulture.

The rhino's bad eyesight was well-known in the jungle. The vultures were not telling Mowgli anything new and startling. Also, the man-cub knew in his bones that they were not trying to help him. Far from it. "You're just trying to start something," the boy accused.

The large vulture wasn't particularly indignant at the charge. "We just want a bit of a happening," he admitted. "We like a bit of a lark!"

The bird seemed to think that Mowgli would completely understand this simple, basic desire. Instead the man-cub shook his head and announced, "Not with me!"

But now Gainda the rhino lifted his nose and tasted the breeze. "I smell a man-cub!" he said. "Where is he? Let me at him!"

Mowgli decided instantly that he would face Kaa, or the monkey king, or even Hathi rather than the clumsy, half-blind monster who now confronted him. Stealthily the boy began to back away.

The vultures didn't think this a bit fair. They had gone to considerable trouble to bring the rhinoceros and the man-cub face to face, and now the boy was trying to cheat them out of their sport.

"He's right over here!" called the large vulture. With an agile hop he got behind Mowgli and spread his wings to block the man-cub's retreat. The other birds crowded around, nearly smothering the boy with their wings.

The rhino approached at an easy lope that fairly shook the ground. "Thanks," he said to the vultures. "I may not see so good, but I smell awful good." And he laughed. The sound was infinitely worse than his roar of rage.

The vultures melted to the rear as the rhino at last came close enough to see the man-cub. Only the largest vulture stayed where he was, effectively cutting off Mowgli's only escape route.

The rhino took an experimental sniff at Mowgli, and the boy cried out, more bravely than circumstances really justified, "Get out of my way!" Then, pleadingly, Mowgli said, "I just want to be left alone."

It was absolutely true. That was all the man-cub desired. But the rhino was not placated. He tore at the earth, marking a line quite close to Mowgli's bare toes. "Just step across that line, man-cub. I dare you!" he challenged.

"What for?" asked Mowgli meekly.

The rhino hadn't expected the question, and he had no answer. "Aw, come on!" he urged. "Please step across!"

"But I'm not mad at you," Mowgli explained. "I just. . . ." He was about to say again that he just wanted to be left alone, but he had no chance. The large vulture stationed behind him lurched forward, sending the boy sprawling across the line.

"He stepped across!" crowed the big bird.

"He stepped across! He stepped across!" chorused the others, anxious that the rhino should take note of this fact.

"Well!" huffed the rhino, happily working himself into a rage. "Well, that does it!"

Then he stopped and looked about in his dim-witted way. "Where is he?" he wanted to know.

As it happened, Mowgli was standing almost under the rhino's nose. He felt a sudden anger that made his face go hot and his neck redden. This mighty rhino, this much-dreaded Gainda, might be big enough, but it was plain to see that his mind was as dull as his vision. And as far as the vultures were concerned, Mowgli vowed to himself that he would not let them put their ugly wings on him once more.

"I am right here!" said the man-cub to the rhino.

"You are?" said the rhino. "Oh, yes. There you are. Well, then, ready or not, here I come!"

Once having focused on Mowgli, the rhino was not going to take his eyes off the man-cub. The giant animal backed away step by step, keeping his gaze fixed on the boy even when Mowgli blurred in his vision.

"Fight! Fight!" shouted the big vulture.

"Yeah!" cheered the others. "Fight! You and him fight!"

"Give him a bit of punch and blow!" advised the big vulture.

The rhino was only too willing. Still staring just as hard as he could at Mowgli, he pounded forward, head low, horn ready.

152

Mowgli ignored the howling vultures and waited until the rhino was quite close. Then the boy leaped easily aside.

The rhino charged on, past Mowgli and into the midst of the screaming birds. The vultures scattered with a wild flapping of wings. One who wasn't quite quick enough encountered the rhino's horn and was tossed, shrieking, into the air.

The rhino stupidly watched the unfortunate bird's tail feathers float down past his nose. "Hey!" he exclaimed. "That man-cub was stuffed with feathers!"

The damaged vulture dragged himself up from the earth a full twenty feet from the rhino. "You stupid idiot!" he croaked.

The rhino was bewildered. He had made a direct hit on the man-cub, hadn't he? Or had he? He had hit someone or something, he knew that. All these feathers had to come from somewhere. "Did I miss him?" asked the rhino plaintively. "Where'd he go?"

"He went that way," said the large vulture. He pointed after Mowgli, who was hurrying away across the plain as fast as he could hurry without actually running.

The rhino could not see the man-cub, but he could

see the extended wing pointing the way to battle. "Aim me at him!" he ordered.

The vultures were happy to do so. It was not easy for them to turn the rhino around, but they managed it with much heaving and flapping of wings. Then the large vulture pressed the rhino's head until it was lowered to charging position. "Now hold it!" counseled the vulture. "You're right on target. Ready! Charge!"

And charge the rhino did, directly at the man-cub.

"Brace yourself, lad!" hooted the plump little vulture.

"I can't watch!" cried the big vulture in mock horror. He shrank back and covered his eyes with his wings.

The other birds thought this terribly amusing, and they, too, pretended to cringe away from the coming slaughter. Some of them turned their backs. Others put their heads under their wings.

So, as it turned out, none saw Mowgli turn toward the charging rhinoceros. And none saw the man-cub slip aside once more, dodging behind one of the many stone outcroppings that dotted the plain. The rhino thundered blindly into the stone. There was a frightful smashing sound, and the rhino slumped to the ground beside the boulder.

"Well," said the large vulture cheerfully, "that's the end of the man-cub. Let's go pick up the pieces."

And he took his wings away from his eyes and looked.

Mowgli had come from behind the rock and was standing above the rhino, watching him nervously.

"Well, I'll be . . ." gasped the vulture.

"That new fellow punched Gainda right off the scene!" exclaimed a second vulture.

It was incredible! It couldn't be true! The man-cub could not possibly have felled the rhinoceros. Yet somehow that is exactly what had happened.

It took the large vulture only a moment to come to a decision. Not everything could work out as planned. And there *had* been a bit of a happening, that was certain. Best to go along with it. "Come on, mates!" he cried. "Let's go meet the new champ!"

But Mowgli wasn't too interested in receiving congratulations from the vultures. The half-stunned rhino had pulled himself to a sitting position. His horn was terribly battered and his poor, nearsighted eyes kept crossing.

155

"Are you all right?" asked Mowgli timidly.

A tear ran from one of the rhino's dim eyes and trickled down to his horn. "You didn't have to hit me so hard," he sniffed.

"Oh, but I didn't . . ." Mowgli began to explain.

"Just look what you did to my horn!" cried the rhino. "You ruined it! Oooh! My poor head!"

Mowgli touched the horn. It wasn't quite what it had been, but it was still more or less intact. "You'll be all right," said the boy, trying to be cheerful.

The rhino shook his head carefully to see if it was still firmly attached to his shoulders. It was. He began to brighten up. "Anyway," he remarked, "I've still got all my marbles."

Mowgli doubted this, but it would have been rude to say so. Besides, the vultures were now swarming around, as hearty in their good wishes as if they had been the man-cub's lifelong friends.

"Say, new guy!" said the big vulture. "We dig you!"

"You're a bit of all right!" applauded another vulture.

"He's got a bit of our breed in him, he has," declared a third bird.

156

"And mine, too," put in the rhinoceros, sadly squinting down at his battered horn.

"Kid," said the big vulture, "we'd like to make you an honorary vulture!"

The big bird waited a moment, then noticed that Mowgli did not seem to be overcome with joy at the idea. "That's an invitation we don't give to everybody, you know," said the vulture.

Mowgli was sure of that, but not all honors could be carelessly accepted. To be a wolf was a noble thing. To be a bear and roam with Baloo would have been a joy. It might not have been bad even to be a monkey, once he got the knack of tree-swinging. But a vulture?

"Thanks very much," said Mowgli, "but I'd rather be on my own." Then, to be sure that the birds completely understood, Mowgli added, "I'd rather be alone."

The vultures were shocked. Alone? Who ever heard of such a thing.

"Alone?" asked the big vulture.

"Alone in the jungle?" said the plump little vulture.

"You're joking, matey!" declared a third vulture.

"Haven't you got any friends?" asked a fourth.

"You must have some mates," cried a fifth bird.

"I haven't," said Mowgli. "Not anymore." Then, thinking that this conversation had gone just about as far as it could go, Mowgli turned toward the green, protective wall of the forest. Better Bagheera and his stuffy ways, or even Hathi and his temper, than these strange creatures crowding around him.

But the large vulture wasn't to be put down that easily. He hopped in front of Mowgli and fluttered his wings. "Wait!" he cried. "Now, look, you've got friends. Sure you have." He turned toward his fellows. "Mates, are we his friends?" he challenged.

"Right!" cried the little fat vulture.

"We sure are!" another bird seconded the motion.

"Friends to the bitter end," vowed a third.

> "When you're done in, who hangs around
> To pluck you up when you are down?"

sang the large vulture. The other birds quickly chimed in:

> "And when you're out for the count,
> Who picks you off the floor?
> A-that, a-that, a-that, a-that,
> A-that's what friends are for!"

It sounded very cozy, but Mowgli knew full well that the birds had simply mastered a way of saying some most unpleasant things in a reasonably pleasant way. Besides, they were circling about him now, doing a hopping, twisting, jerking little dance, and brushing at his toes and his bare knees with the tips of their wings. He shrank back from them and felt the rough, solid bulk of the rhinoceros behind him.

"You know the zebra, the hyena, and
the kangaroo,
The cobra, and the lion all agree it's true!"

croaked the birds.

"We're fond of every creature comin' down
the pike.
In fact, we've never met an animal we
didn't like!
So you can see, we're friends in need,
And friends in need are friends indeed!
We'll keep you safe in the jungle
forevermore!
A-that, a-that, a-that, a-that,
A-that's what friends are for!"

The birds were fluttering faster and faster, more and more wildly. Mowgli scrambled up out of the way, onto the back of the now docile rhino.

"We're your friends!" shouted the largest of the vultures.

"We're your friends!" chorused the others, leaping madly in time to the music. "We're your friends to the bitter end!"

The song went on and on and on, and the dance became more and more frenzied. Even the rhino swayed to the rhythm of the big birds. Mowgli clung to his perch, half-frightened and half-fascinated by the strange chant.

Then a wildly capering shadow fell across the dancers. It was a very large shadow—much too large for a vulture. Mowgli lifted his head and stared.

"Hey, dig him!" chortled one of the vultures.

"Beat the turf, matey!" cheered another.

"Get him! Look at old dad!" cried a third.

"Who?" cried the poor blind rhino. "Get who? What old dad?"

No one bothered to answer. Mowgli was too surprised and the vultures were far too busy urging on Baloo. The bear had, as usual, been completely unable to resist a chance to dance.

"He's kind of big," crowed the plump vulture, "but he sure can swing it!"

"You'd better believe it!" gasped Baloo the bear.

11.
Shere Khan

BAGHEERA the panther crouched under a thornbush at the edge of the jungle and wished with all his heart that he was elsewhere.

"Disgraceful!" he said to himself. "Shocking! Utterly incredible!"

Baloo, if he was at all aware of the panther's disapproval, gave no sign. He went right on capering in the sunlight while the vultures jeered and whooped and Mowgli watched. And when the sun hid behind a bank of clouds and a rumble of thunder sounded across the plain, Baloo only danced harder.

"Too much!" declared Bagheera bitterly. "He's entirely too much! Consorting with carrion eaters! Ugh!"

Bagheera would gladly have taken himself away—away from the dead tree and the black pool and the weirdly strutting vultures—if only he could. But he couldn't. He couldn't return to Council Rock to confess to the wolves that he had abandoned the man-cub to the care of a flock of vultures plus one idiot bear. Bagheera had given his word. He had promised to take Mowgli to the man-village, and he intended to do it.

It was plain to see, however, that he could not be about this task immediately. Sooner or later the dancers would tire. Then Bagheera would move in and speak his words of wisdom, and Baloo and Mowgli would listen to him. In the meantime, Bagheera closed his eyes to shut out the painful sight of the bear dancing to the vulture's tune.

The panther did not see Shere Khan.

For two days the tiger had stalked with the scent of the man-cub ever stronger in his nostrils. Now the hunt was ending. Shere Khan skirted the thornbush under which the panther waited. He noted the presence of

Bagheera and then dismissed the panther from his mind. Bagheera would not interfere. He was far too wise to try to come between Shere Khan and his prey.

The tiger flattened himself in the tall grass at the edge of the plain and waited. There was no hurry. This time the man-cub could not escape. This time there was no den in which he could be hidden, no Raksha to leap to his defense with bared fangs. There was only foolish old Baloo, who was hardly a problem, and the vultures, who were beneath notice. And there was Mowgli, the hated man-cub, half-grown now, but still helpless. Too sure for caution, Shere Khan allowed a rumbling purr of pure pleasure to escape from him.

Thunder cracked above the tiger, and lightning forked down to blast a tree somewhere in the depths of the jungle. The tiger did not even turn his head. The storm was not important. What was important was on the plain before him. He inched forward, creeping low, scarcely stirring the grass as he went. Then, when he was within a few feet of the dancers, he roared and sprang.

The vultures moved more quickly than the lightning that split the sky. One instant they were all around

Mowgli and Baloo, laughing and singing. The next, they had all swooped away to the dead tree.

Gainda the rhino moved, too, first shrugging Mowgli from his back, then lumbering in a confused half-circle, and at last taking himself off to cower behind a rock.

Only Baloo and Mowgli remained to face Shere Khan. Baloo was frozen in midstep, one foot off the ground, staring dazedly at the tiger.

"Shere Khan!" he gasped finally.

"Shere Khan!" Mowgli echoed inwardly. It was he! It was Shere Khan, the dreaded one!

The man-cub looked about in panic. He must run! He must hide! But there was no place to hide. Mowgli closed his eyes then and waited for the death blow. And when it did not come, he looked again at Shere Khan. The tiger was watching him with leisurely anticipation.

"Shere Khan!" breathed Baloo again. Then the bear managed to get hold of himself. "It's . . . er . . . nice to see you again, Shere Khan," he said, attempting a pleasant conversational tone.

Shere Khan ignored this blatant untruth.

"Er . . . Little Britches and me," began Baloo again,

"we're just on our way to the man-village."

The bear took Mowgli's hand in his huge paw and began to walk away with the boy.

"Not so fast," snarled Shere Khan. "I want the man-cub."

Baloo quickly put Mowgli behind him.

"I mean it, Baloo!" said Shere Khan. "I've waited a long time for this moment. Don't get in the way or you'll regret it."

"Aw, come on!" protested Baloo. "What do you have against the kid here? He's never done anything to you."

"He's a man!" snapped Shere Khan.

"Just a cub," Baloo reminded the tiger. "And once I get him to the man-village, you'll never see him again."

"Of course not," replied the tiger. "Not until he's grown and has a gun and the red flower. I'll see him then! He will come looking for me." The tiger's huge shoulders twitched, and Baloo saw the place which was scarred and hairless. Even now, years after the night Shere Khan had hunted in the fields near the man-village, the wound looked angry.

"Get out of the way, Baloo!" warned the tiger. "I'm

not going to wait for the cub to grow and be a man. I'm going to stop him now!"

Baloo stood his ground. "You big bully," he stormed. "You're something, aren't you, going after Little Britches here. Why don't you pick on someone your own size?"

The tiger smiled a sly smile. "My own size?" he said. "What an interesting idea! Wouldn't you say that you're about my size, Baloo?"

The bear hadn't meant it quite that way. He started to back off, pushing Mowgli behind him. "Aw, now, Shere Khan," he protested, "I don't think. . . ."

The tiger came erect, every muscle tensed. "You asked for it, Baloo," he told the bear. "Let's go!"

Baloo had time only to push Mowgli to one side before he met the tiger's charge.

"You show him, Baloo!" shouted Mowgli. "Weave and duck! Give him the old footwork! Give him—"

Before Mowgli could tell Baloo what else he was to give the tiger, a black flash crossed the field. Bagheera seized the man-cub firmly by the breechcloth and began to drag him away.

"Stop!" roared the tiger. "Bagheera! Don't you dare take him! He's mine!"

Shere Khan turned from Baloo and started after the panther.

"No you don't!" cried the bear. He seized the tiger's tail and tugged for all he was worth.

The tiger spun about, raging, and Baloo stumbled backward, still tugging, trying desperately to keep the tail taut, to keep his distance from those cruel fangs and the unsheathed claws.

Bagheera wasted no time watching to see how the tug-of-war progressed. He carried the struggling, kicking man-cub to a tree at the edge of the jungle, plumped him down hard on the ground, and stood over him.

"Let me go!" cried Mowgli. "Get out of the way, Bagheera. We have to help Baloo!"

"You can't help Baloo, foolish man-cub," warned the panther. "Now, get up and run for your life!"

"I can't!" shouted Mowgli. "I won't!"

"You must!" commanded Bagheera. "Quick now, get up and—"

A deafening blast of thunder cut the panther's words short. There was a flash that seared Mowgli's eyes as lightning struck the tree above them. The man-cub thought for a moment that the world was on fire, that

it was burning all around him. Then the fire went dark and, for a little time, the boy knew nothing more.

When Mowgli wakened, the red flower still bloomed in the tree above him. Beside him Bagheera was very, very still. And in the field beyond the pool, Shere Khan stood triumphant above the body of Baloo.

The tiger looked up. He looked directly into the eyes of the boy. "Now it's your turn, man-cub," he said. His voice was rough with hatred.

There was no time to think of Bagheera or Baloo. There was no time to think at all. Mowgli only knew that the red flower was near at hand. Its sparks were falling around him. The man-cub scrambled up, clutched at the burning tree, and tugged with all his might. A blazing brand came away in his hand. Holding it awkwardly before him, he began to run— not away, as Bagheera had counseled, but *toward* the tiger.

Shere Khan lowered his head and stepped back nervously. "Put that down, man-cub," he commanded.

The flame at the end of the wood leaped and was mirrored in the big cat's eyes.

"I said put it down," snarled Shere Khan.

Mowgli laughed.

The laugh infuriated the tiger. For an instant the man-cub thought the cat would leap, fire or no fire. But Shere Khan saw the red flower dancing before his eyes and remembered a long-ago night. The old wound in his shoulder throbbed. He did not leap. Instead, to Mowgli's astonishment, he drew in his breath and blew at the burning brand as hard as he could.

For a hideous second the flame disappeared. The great muscles beneath the gold and black hide gathered to spring. Then the red flower bloomed again, stronger than ever, and the tiger groaned and turned away his head.

"Coward!" taunted Mowgli. He stepped forward to dash the flame at the tiger. His foot came down hard on a stone and he stumbled. The red flower fell in a shower of sparks.

"Very well, man-cub!" growled Shere Khan. He began to circle the flame to get at Mowgli. His eyes gleamed with a green fire of their own.

Mowgli bent and snatched up the brand just in time. Again he held it between himself and the tiger.

Shere Khan flinched and shrank back. "You'll burn yourself with that, little one," he whined. "Put it down before it's too late."

Again Mowgli laughed. "I am a man," he said proudly. "Men do not fear the red flower. Only cowards like you, Shere Khan, are afraid!"

Again Mowgli made as if to dash the flames into the tiger's face.

"No, no!" moaned Shere Khan. He crouched and put his great head on his paws. "Spare me, man-cub."

"Do you think I'm a fool?" demanded Mowgli. "If I spare you today, you'll hunt me again tomorrow."

"I won't," promised the tiger. "I'll go away. I'll go back to the north. You'll never see me again!"

"Do you promise?"

"I give the word of Shere Khan!" said the tiger. And the tiger crept forward to lick the boy's feet.

"Run away, coward!" commanded Mowgli.

Shere Khan went then, without looking back. In a twinkling the jungle had swallowed him up.

Mowgli dropped the blazing piece of wood. It had begun to burn his fingers.

12.
Mowgli's Triumph

I SAW YOU, man-cub."

The black panther had come to stand quietly beside Mowgli. The brand still burned at the boy's feet, but it was sputtering now. Soon it would die.

"I saw you," repeated Bagheera.

Mowgli put his hand on the panther's head. "I thought you were dead," he said softly.

Bagheera cleared his throat in that important way he had. "Not quite," he told Mowgli. "Just stunned. I saw you drive Shere Khan away. I . . . I would not have believed it, otherwise."

"Will he stay away?" asked Mowgli.

Bagheera considered this question with his usual care. "I should think so," he said at last. "He gave his word. So you have little more to worry about, eh, man-cub?"

"Except Baloo," said Mowgli. He felt that he would cry, and he didn't want to. Not now.

"Ah, Baloo!" Bagheera looked toward the motion-less body of the bear. Then he looked toward the vul-tures' tree. One of the big birds had started to fly up from the tree, but he caught the panther's glance and hastily returned to his perch.

Together Mowgli and Bagheera approached Baloo's still form.

Mowgli knelt and lifted the bear's shaggy head onto his knees. The battering the bear had received from the monkeys was nothing compared to the destruction accomplished by Shere Khan. "Oh, Bagheera!" said Mowgli. "Is he . . . is he. . . ."

"Dead?" finished the panther. He looked closely at Baloo. Not a muscle in the bear's body twitched. "I'm afraid so," said Bagheera sadly. "It's . . . it's to be expected, of course. He knew when he defied Shere

Khan that this would happen."

"And he went ahead and did it anyway." A tear slid down Mowgli's cheek and dropped from his chin onto the bear's nose.

"He went ahead and did it anyway," echoed Bagheera. "He was your true friend, man-cub. A bit foolish at times, perhaps. Not very dignified. But a true friend. No one could have greater love than his. He laid down his own life to save yours."

"Oh, Baloo!" sobbed Mowgli. He cradled the big head in his arms.

To Mowgli's surprise, one of Baloo's eyes twitched. Then it opened, as bright and funny as ever. And then it winked a conspiratorial wink at Mowgli.

"There—" said Bagheera, in his most solemn tone, "there lies one of the earth's noblest creatures!"

"You'd better believe it!" rumbled Baloo.

"Oh, Baloo!" cried Mowgli. Then he laughed. Then he cried. Then he laughed again and hugged the bear, who sat up and hugged him back.

"Good heavens!" gasped Bagheera. "Baloo! You're all right! You're not dead!"

Mowgli hugged Baloo the bear again, harder than ever.

"You'd better believe it," laughed Baloo.

"I'll never, never leave you again, Baloo!" vowed Mowgli.

"Ha-ha! That's my boy!" The bear was enjoying himself enormously.

Bagheera started to say something profound about the importance of returning the man-cub to his own people, but he thought better of it and closed his mouth. It was embarrassing enough to be caught delivering a funeral oration for a very live companion. Certainly neither Baloo nor Mowgli would thank him for dampening their joyous reunion with talk of parting.

"But, hey!" said Baloo suddenly. "What happened to Old Stripes?"

"Shere Khan?" said Bagheera. "Mowgli drove him away."

"He did?" Baloo thought well of Mowgli, but he hadn't realized that the man-cub was that talented. "How?" asked the bear.

"With the red flower," Bagheera explained. He nodded toward the lightning-struck tree, now smoking and sputtering as the flames died out in its blackened branches.

178

"That's my boy!" chortled Baloo. He ruffled Mowgli's hair with his paw.

"Shere Khan will not return," Bagheera announced. "He gave his word."

"That's a break for everybody!" said Baloo with relief.

"Now nothing can ever come between us," declared Mowgli happily. "I can stay in the jungle with you forever and ever."

"Even longer than that, if you want," agreed the bear. "What about that, Bagheera?"

The panther sighed. It seemed that the man-cub had won after all. He had driven away the tiger. And when news of this spread through the jungle, as it would, even Kaa would hesitate to lie in wait for him. But what of the bandar-log? What would the monkey king do when he learned that the man-cub had used the red flower? Most important of all, what of Mowgli himself. "I am a man!" he had told Shere Khan, and it was true, though neither he nor silly Baloo would admit it now.

But Bagheera could argue no more. There was nothing to be gained by argument. Perhaps there was another way.

"I think," he said at last, "that it should be up to the man-cub."

"There you go!" said Baloo happily.

"One might say that he has proved himself," Bagheera announced.

"One sure might," declared Baloo.

"Of course," said the cunning panther, "it would be rather a shame to come so far and not see it."

"See what, Bagheera?" Mowgli asked.

"Why, that man-village, of course," Bagheera told him. "We're quite near it now. Oh, I don't think you should go *into* it, but you just might want to take a look—a glance or two from the edge of the jungle. After all, you were born there."

"I know," said Mowgli.

"Hey, why not, Little Britches?" asked the bear. "I'd kind of like to see it myself."

"Well," said Mowgli, "all right. But just a look, that's all. I'm not going in."

"Of course you're not," said Bagheera soothingly. "No need to now, is there?"

"No need at all," said Mowgli firmly.

And with that happily decided, the panther, the bear, and the man-cub started off through the jungle.

Mowgli and Baloo sang about how a bear can live at ease with just the bare necessities of life.

Bagheera did not sing. But he led the way, and he was smiling.

13.
The Man-Village

Look for the bare necessities," sang Baloo.

"The simple bare necessities," Mowgli warbled.

"Come on, Baggy, get with it," urged Baloo. " 'Forget about your worries and your strife.' Try that line."

"Do be quiet, Baloo!" snapped the panther.

"Huh?" said Baloo. Everything had been going along so chirpily. Now what was the matter with old fret-and-fuss?

"We're nearly there," explained Bagheera. He pointed ahead to a place where the trees thinned and they could see the sky. "Their fields are just beyond those trees." His voice had dropped nearly to a whisper.

Mowgli started to run ahead, but Bagheera cautioned him with a hissed, "Sssh! Keep low and don't make any noise!"

"But Mowgli doesn't need to worry," Baloo pointed out. "They're not going to come after him with guns and the red flower. He's a man-cub."

"But we are not," was Bagheera's acid reply.

"Oh!" said Baloo. "Oh, yeah! Sure. I didn't think of that!"

"Bagheera!" Mowgli was down on his knees peering across the fields toward the place where a mud wall enclosed a cluster of thatch-roofed houses. "Bagheera, come and look!"

"I've seen it," said Bagheera. But he went just the same, and Baloo went with him.

"Are those their dens?" Mowgli asked, pointing to the roofs.

"That is where the men sleep," said Bagheera in his precise way. "They are called huts, or houses, depending upon the size, I believe. The men make them out of sticks and mud."

"It must be a lot of work," mumbled Baloo. "It'd be easier just to sleep under a tree."

"Or in a cave," added Mowgli.

"Men prefer not to sleep under trees or in caves," Bagheera said. "They feel safe only in their huts."

"That's silly," said Baloo.

"It's their custom," Bagheera pointed out.

Baloo was silent. A custom was a custom and not to be argued with. The birds lived in the trees and the lizards scuttled among the stones on the ground, and who could say that either was mistaken?

"The red flower is in the village," Mowgli said. A wisp of smoke curled up from among the houses.

"The red flower is always in the village," explained Bagheera. "It is the servant of man. It does many things for him."

"Like driving away Shere Khan?" asked Mowgli.

"That, of course," conceded Bagheera. "And it keeps man warm at night and cooks his food. . . ."

"Cooks?" questioned Mowgli. He had not heard this word before.

Bagheera smiled. "Man is a peculiar creature, as you will learn," he told Mowgli. "He does not eat his food as it comes to him, but instead he puts it into the red flower until it is very hot. Then he eats it."

"That's funny," laughed Baloo. "I wonder how burnt bananas taste."

"We could try them some time, Baloo," suggested Mowgli.

"No, thanks," said Baloo hastily. "I'm not fooling around with any red flower. Not this old bear."

"Are the men all inside their houses now?" Mowgli asked. "I don't see any."

"Probably," said Bagheera. "The night is coming. At night they stay inside their walls."

"Gee, Baggy," said Baloo, "how come you know so much about them?"

"They interest me," said Bagheera loftily. "Everything interests me. And one can learn a great deal by walking softly and wearing the same color as the night."

"Oh, yeah!" muttered the bear, who generally charged through life making as much uproar as possible. "Yeah, sure!"

"Oh, there's one!" Mowgli whispered. He pointed to the gate in the village wall. A little girl came out and started across the fields to the place where a small stream ran down.

"Uh . . . Bagheera, that is one, isn't it?" said Mowgli uncertainly. He had never seen anything like this child. She was dressed in a loose, flowing garment, and her long black hair was caught back from her face in braids that hung down on either side. She was about Mowgli's age, or perhaps a bit younger.

"That's a girl-cub," Bagheera explained. "She lives in the man-village."

"You didn't tell me about those," said Mowgli. He watched with fascination as the girl reached the stream and bent to dip up water into a huge earthen jar which she carried under her arm.

Baloo was suddenly uneasy. "Aww!" he growled. "Girl-cubs are nothing but trouble!"

Mowgli didn't even pretend to pay any attention to this. "I'm going to have a better look," he said brightly, and he started to step out onto the cleared field.

"Mowgli!" cried Baloo. "Don't do it!"

"Oh, I'll be right back," Mowgli assured him. "Wait for me."

He went on toward the girl, who now knelt beside the stream at a place where a tree hung over a little natural basin and the water became smooth and still for a time before running on again down the slope.

The girl was singing, watching herself in the water, smoothing her plaited hair with her fingers. Mowgli could not understand her words, but her voice was marvelously soft.

> "Father's hunting in the forest.
> Mother's cooking in the home.
> I must go to fetch the water
> Till the day that I am grown,"

she sang.

Mowgli watched from the far side of the stream. She knew that he was there, for once she looked up and then looked away quickly.

> "Then I'll have a handsome husband,"

her song went on.

> "And a daughter of my own,
> And I'll send her to fetch the water.
> I'll be cooking in the home."

Her hair was arranged to her own satisfaction now and her water jar was full. Without looking again in Mowgli's direction she stood up, raised the jar to the top of her head, and, balancing the weight easily with one hand, started back toward the village.

Mowgli stood motionless, watching her go. At the edge of the jungle, Baloo felt his heart give a happy thump. That would be the end of it. Let her go!

But that was not the end of it. Mowgli looked up at the vines that dangled from the tree above the pool. To Baloo's horror he grasped one of them, swung himself across the pool and began turning cartwheels in the path in front of the girl-cub.

When he had turned ten cartwheels and added a somersault or two to his performance, he stopped long enough to ask the girl-cub her name.

"She can't understand him," whispered Baloo to Bagheera.

"I wouldn't worry." The panther chuckled. "I imagine she understands well enough when a man-cub starts acting like that."

Indeed, the girl-cub seemed perfectly at ease in the situation. She did what any well-bred girl-cub would do. She giggled. Then she handed her water jar to Mowgli and walked on. And Mowgli, after standing and wondering for a second or two, walked after her across the fields. Just before he went through the gate into the man-village, he looked back and waved once.

Then he was gone. Bagheera and Baloo could see him no longer.

For a time Baloo was silent. Then he sighed a mighty sigh. "That must be one of those necessities," he said sadly.

"That's right, Baloo," Bagheera agreed. "Like goes to like."

Baloo sighed again. "I still think he'd make one swell bear."

Bagheera didn't reply, and after a bit Baloo stood up and shook himself. "Oh, well," he said, "no sense in waiting around here, I guess. Come on, Baggy! On your feet!"

Bagheera was pleased enough to get up. It was easy to be agreeable when one has been proved right. Still, things wouldn't be quite the same without the man-cub.

"I must remember to tell Hathi that we found Mowgli," said Bagheera happily.

"Aw, why bother?" replied Baloo. "He's probably having a great time looking for the kid. Come on, Baggy, help me finish the song we started, and this time, get with the beat!"

So Baloo and Bagheera retreated into the jungle.

Had their man-cub been watching, which he was not, he would have seen that the panther was singing and dancing along with the bear. He was a bit stiff and awkward about it, but his intentions were the best. Bagheera, at last, was getting with the beat.

Or at least he was trying.